COUSINS' BAD BLOOD

Power-Sex-Money-Murder-Deception

Date: 10/27/15

LAC FIC BERRI
Berri, Fred,
Cousins' bad blood :power...sex...
money...murder...deception

fred berri

ISBN: 1508567298
ISBN 13: 9781508567295
Library of Congress Control Number: 2015902917
CreateSpace Independent Publishing Platform
North Charleston, South Carolina

This story is fictional. Any names, places, or situations are a fougasse[1] and are purely coincidental with the exception of historical events, historical names, historical dates, or any actual location(s).

To
Lola,
the love of my life
(most days)

PROLOGUE

CHARLES NICHOLAS PELL remembers how it was growing up in the Bronx, New York. It was easy. It was fun. There was always a challenge and always —yes, always—something to do and someone to do it with. He grew up as Charlie Pell and was first-generation Italian American on his father's side and second-generation Italian American on his mother's side—this according to his father, Michael, who came from a small province in Italy called Avellino in the region known as Campania.

He recalled his father telling stories, sipping espresso while sitting around the dining room table, where most Italian families spent a great deal of time. He spoke with great detail and never a wasted word, waving his hands to describe the beauty in the mountains and hills, in the people, and in their culture and family values.

Every story ended with his lips kissing the tips of his fingers, raising them, looking toward the sky, smiling, and saying, *"Il mio cuore e bacio per due."*

It was his heart and a kiss for two, his parents, who sacrificed everything for him.

Charlie found out many years later that his father, when coming to this country in March 1906 at the age of twelve, had a different name: Michael Pellegrino.

What Charlie didn't know was why his father changed his name from Pellegrino to Pell and how he became one of the most powerful men in America.

But there was always the rumor.

Book One

The New World

CHAPTER 1

FROM THE MOMENT Michael Pellegrino set foot on Ellis Island in 1906, where all immigrants were processed, he knew he wanted people to respect him. Doctors were probing the new arrivals, and authorities were pushing them to stand behind the line. Everyone was scared, alone, and confused. After fourteen days at sea in steerage, the area below water level where it was always dark and shared by livestock—conditions were unsanitary, causing sickness among the passengers—many were sick from the overcrowding. They all welcomed the sight of land and the opportunity to set foot on America's soil. Michael spent as much of the journey as he could asleep. When he wasn't sleeping, he was wandering the ship's deck with his family just for the fresh air. A vision that would always stay in Michael's mind was seeing his mother vomiting over the rail most of the fourteen days while he stood painfully quiet, watching, as his father held her, keeping her warm.

Officials were shouting, "Wops, over here," giving meaning to with-out papers

Michael already missed the mountains of his homeland. He even missed the hard work of helping his uncle on the farm. Now, the new vision that met his eyes was of huge buildings and people speaking many new languages. He didn't know what they were saying, but he knew what they were laughing about: him and his fellow Italians, the way they were dressed. They held their noses to give the "stink" sign.

In Michael's mind was rattling, *Vorrei avere in mio potere per non permettere a nessuno di questo tipo di beffardo di me o la mia famiglia*. He knew he didn't have it in his power to stop anyone from mocking him or his family—at least for the moment.

Growing up in an Italian family, you were always taught family was the most important thing. Even at the tender age of twelve, Michael knew he was going to demand respect—for himself, his family, and his future children. Michael grew up fast, in a section of Manhattan known as Little Italy, an ethnic area where most Italians settled. The narrow streets of cobblestone gave the flavor of the homeland.

CHAPTER 2

WHEN YOU IMMIGRATED to America, you had to contribute to society. It was required that you be sponsored by someone established in the United States.

Michael's father and mother were sponsored by a distant cousin who had been in America a few years and who was considered "established." He got Michael's father a job at the train yards at the Bronx Terminal Market. He got Michael's mother a job as a seamstress in a sweatshop located on the Lower East Side of Manhattan. The conditions were terrible, thus the term *sweatshop*. One hundred women sat shoulder to shoulder, row after row. You could smell the bad breath of the person sitting next to you. The stench of body odor permeated the small factory room, which was located on the third-level of a walk-up loft building. During summer months, the windows were wide open and fans blew in hot air. It didn't stop the sweat dripping from foreheads and underarms.

During winter months, the same windows were open and the same fans were blowing. This time it was to help keep the stench to a minimum. The cold outside temperatures helped to replace the stale air. The fans battled constantly with the steam bellowing from the radiators, which filled the room with heat. Permeating it all was the smell of unbathed bodies. There were no winners in this battle. There was no controlling the steam provided by the landlord. There was no controlling the cold outside temperature.

The sewing machines never stopped buzzing because the workers were paid by how many pieces they were able to seam together by the end of day. Their heads were always leaning forward; arms perched atop the machines, guiding every stich. Many would not even get up to relieve themselves, but rather, they had a bucket next to them to urinate into. The bosses puffed cigars that only added to the stuffy air. They wore shirts, ties, and vests and would walk the floor, watching everything, especially the finished pieces, falling into bins next to each girl. Many of the seamstresses were young girls. Some were as young as twelve years old. All of them knew that if they didn't keep pace, they would be out of a job, and there would be as many as a hundred women looking to take their place.

Michael's parents worked hard and long to be successful in their new country, just like all the immigrants who came to America. Many immigrants could not take what they had to face and did not think it was worth it. Some returned to their homeland. Some committed suicide. But others found the streets paved with gold. Michael wanted to stay in America. He knew that, as much as he missed his homeland country, family, and farm, he wanted to have some of the gold that was paving the streets.

He saw that by working hard, you could own your own business, as many immigrants were able to do. There were butcher shops, shoemaker shops, and grocery stores all along the cobblestone streets of Little Italy. It took years of hard work and saving every penny to achieve the goal of owning your own business, but in the end, those hardworking people were respected and proud of what they were able to accomplish.

Michael began scowling and sighing at the same time, uttering, "*Voglio quella. Mi metterò quello!*" He knew what he wanted and was determined he woud get exactly what he set out to accomplish.

CHAPTER 3

MICHAEL WAS A tough kid who quickly grasped the new language and the ins and outs of the New World. He had a few scuffles with other kids. While he always walked away victorious, he could be heard mumbling, "*Devo lottare per ogni fottuto centimetro*[1] He wasn't going to let anyone get in his way. On one occasion, he hit an older and bigger kid so hard that a knuckle on Michael's left hand moved. He knocked the kid unconscious and broke his jaw, earning himself a reputation in the neighborhood as a tough leader.

The years that followed were the years that shaped Michael, his emotions and desires, through long, hard work. He adapted to the New World's ways, encountering both celebrations and disappointments.

His mother died from tuberculosis, a common cause of death during that time. There were the unsanitary conditions of tenement housing, the overcrowding on the streets, in the sweatshops, and even at home, as his family lived together to share their living quarters and expenses. There were few doctor visits, if any. Michael, however, was a survivor. Many individuals who knew Michael thought it was an uncertain time for him. But as these conditions continued year after year, Michael did not lose any clarity of his goals. In fact, his goals took on even greater importance.

His father, missing his mother, began to wane rapidly. He would work long hours most days without a break. Many times he would stop on his way home to throw down a few whiskeys with his working buddies.

One particular night, Michael's father didn't make it home. It was not a night of drinking. It was the night he was killed. He was a loader at the Bronx

---

1 I have to fight for every fucking inch.

Terminal Market, where part of his job was to hitch the boxcars together. The accident report indicated that two of the cars were not properly coupled.

Michael had to move in with distant relatives and worked at odd jobs to help pay for his room and board. Everyone living there had to kick in to help pay his share—up and out early each morning to shine shoes, make deliveries, sell newspapers, or stock beer at the local bar. There was no free ride. It didn't matter what it was; you just had to make money.

As grateful as Michael was, he saw clearly how he wanted to mold his own future differently—no schlepping for others, only for himself and his future family. He often thought of his parents and would visit the cemetery every chance he could. Kneeling in front of the simple grave marker with some flowers, making the sign of the cross, Michael would utter, "*Mi mancate. Vi voglio bene—maybe better. Grazie.*"[2]

All the families would donate to help bury friends and family in simple pine boxes. They knew their time would come, and they too would need a simple pine box.

There was much romanticizing about his father's death. It was said that because he mourned his beautiful wife and wanted desperately to be with her, he deliberately did not hook up the coupling on the boxcars the correct way. It is typical of Italians to look deep into the soul of love, like Quasimodo and Esmeralda in *The Hunchback of Notre-Dame*. Amid all the poverty, hardships, hard work, wine, and miserable living conditions, the Italians were always able see the dreamy romanticism in tragedy.

---

2   I miss you. I love you. Thank you.

CHAPTER 4

IN SPITE OF the fact that Michael had limited schooling in Italy, he was now earning his way through life in the New World with New World savvy. He was streetwise and alert to all counseling from friends and relatives. These qualities helped him land a job at Cappelli and Sons. Being very capable in English, Italian, and math, his abilities were quite welcome. He was now eighteen.

Cappelli and Sons was a large grocery, butcher, and imported cheese store on Mott Street in Lower Manhattan. On any given day, there would be prosciutto, sopressata, sausages, salami, and cheeses hanging, filling the air with an aroma that engulfed your taste buds with excitement. The ceiling was carefully crafted with tin, a cheap way to make a sophisticated interior design.

Nicholas Cappelli had had to do what every immigrant had to do to reach the status of owning his own business: work smarter, harder, and longer. Michael knew this work ethic early on and applied it every day as his mantra, never grimacing, always smiling: "Work smarter, harder, and longer, and never take a day off."

Old Man Cappelli didn't have any sons, which he had hoped for, even incorporating it into the store's name. But as fate would have it, Mrs. Cappelli, known as Mama, had three daughters, Regina, Maria, and Theresa, all born in America. The moment Michael laid his eyes on Regina, he began whispering to himself, "*Per Dio, sono stato colpito da un fulmine.*" He knew he'd been struck by lightning.

The days and years seemed to fold into one. He studied Old Man Cappelli and how he dealt with customers, vendors, invoices, deliveries, and family. Mr. Cappelli would clamor during the day: "Maria, take care of Mrs. Garibaldi."

"Mama, don't pay that invoice yet." "Michael, check that delivery before signing for it."

Michael watched the young Cappelli girls grow into young women. As Michael himself grew into a young man, he took more notice of Regina. She was the same age as Michael, and her big, brown eyes and long, auburn hair were strikingly beautiful. Michael saw poetry in motion when Regina moved about the store. She was always quick to smile when she saw Michael. When her father was busy with other business, they would steal moments together and have small conversations.

"Michael, you're a hard worker. Papa says it all the time. He wishes you were his son," said Regina, flirting.

"Then you'd be my sister," muttered Michael, smiling, as he continued up the ladder, stocking the shelves. Every once in a while, they would catch Old Man Cappelli's eye and would immediately go back to what they were doing, in separate parts of the store, of course.

Michael would do everything he possibly could to learn in the store, knowing he was going to apply the knowledge in the future—with the exception of cutting and butchering meat. With squinting eyes and curled nose, he always said, "The butcher always smells like fresh kill and blood. I don't want to go home smelling like that, ever!"

CHAPTER 5

THE SUN ROSE and set a thousand times. Whether blistering-hot summer or freezing winter days, Michael went to work murmuring, "Work smarter, harder, and longer."

Michael was getting restless in life and restless working for Old Man Cappelli. He knew that no matter how much Mr. Cappelli said he wished Michael were his son, Michael would never be able to take over the Cappelli store. After all, there was Mama Cappelli, Regina, Theresa, and Maria, and Mr. Cappelli's brother, Freddy— family, blood... *la famiglia*.

Now twenty-one years old, Michael was eager to be his own man. He knew the time was right to go out on his own. He had savings he had accumulated from working for Nicholas Cappelli and working all those odd jobs all those years. Yes, the time was right. He decided to start his future applying his mantra, "Work smarter, harder, and longer."

Michael began his own business, M.P. Produce Expeditors. He opened a small office at the seaport on South Street. It was strategically located, as the city of New York had just completed the new train yard. It would be there that the ships would unload their goods, and via the rails out of the train yard, the goods would be sent all across America. Michael was excited to put to use all his years of planning. He had many contacts, since for years he'd kept his own ledger of vendors and customers who came and went in Cappelli's store.

The Cappelli family was going to miss such a hard, conscientious worker, particularly knowing his interest in Regina. Mr. Cappelli, being very generous and knowing how hard Michael contributed to his business, gave him an envelope with one hundred dollars, which was equal to almost two month's pay.

"Mr. Cappelli," Michael stammered sheepishly.

"Michael, shh! Take this and put it to good use. Don't say anything. Between you and me, *capito?*"

"*Grazie mille. Metterò a frutto*, Mr. Cappelli. I understand. Thank you very much. "

"*Non essere un straniero s, Michael.*"

"I'll never be a stranger to you or your family, Mr. Cappelli."

Michael made sure he used the word *family* to include everyone in the Cappelli family, especially Regina. Everyone gathered around to wish him good luck. Mrs. Cappelli embraced this beautiful man with hazel eyes, standing taller than most men. It was an adoring hug. Maria and Theresa were properly polite.

Regina seemed to hold Michael a little longer than everyone else as she whispered in his ear, "I'm glad you're not my brother." She felt his heart beating fast against her own chest.

Just as many young immigrants, Michael had the drive to succeed. He knew he would. He now had his own business, M.P. Produce Expeditors. He had the Cappelli family's blessing. And he had his mantra, "Work smarter, harder, and longer."

CHAPTER 6

M.P. PRODUCE EXPEDITOR'S first contract was three boxcars of Florida oranges to be sold to vendors in New York. One of the contacts Michael made while working for Old Man Cappelli was Isaiah Solomon, known to everyone as Izzy. Izzy helped Michael negotiate his first contract, and the two became close friends over the years. Izzy saw something in Michael that was enterprising, and he wanted to be part of it someway, somehow.

Both Michael and Izzy took a train to Florida to buy fresh oranges and to oversee transporting the shipment back to New York.

Michael knew that when they arrived at the yard at South Street, all the vendors would be clamoring for the best-looking merchandise. Damaged goods could be used against M.P. Produce Expeditors.

On the trip back from Florida to New York, Michael and Izzy spent all their waking hours opening crates and rearranging the oranges. They put the best oranges on top. This ensured that M.P. Produce Expeditor's shipment would be the best.

CHAPTER 7

THE MOMENT FINALLY arrived when the long line of boxcars slowly pulled into the yard. The engineer applied the brakes, and they bellowed a screeching sound of metal on metal. Michael was ready. There was a *bam, bam, bam*, rhythm, repeated over and over again, as the yardmen used long, metal rods to release the crossbars that secured the boxcar doors. He had to put the sights and sounds out of his mind. They reminded him of his father's fatal accident that had taken place in a train yard similar to this one.

The doors slid open. "A dollar fifty," yelled the vendors, vying for the best deal for their shops.

"For a full crate of oranges? Are you fucking nuts?" Izzy cried out. "These have been kissed by God." Izzy and his parents emigrated from Israel and settled in Borough Park, Brooklyn. His parents were devoted Hassidic Jews,[1] and Izzy attended the synagogue (*shul*) with them regularly.

In spite of that, Izzy never did warm up to God. He'd always questioned why his people were chosen by God but others were not. He always said, "That's fucked up." He'd refused to have a bar mitzvah when he turned thirteen years old. According to Jewish law, when a Jewish son reaches thirteen years old, he becomes morally and ethically accountable for his actions and has the same rights as a full-grown man. This is marked by the traditional religious ceremony known as a *bar mitzvah*. However, Izzy had refused to become accountable to this God he didn't know and didn't understand, so he would not participate in anything having to do with his bar

---

1 Hasidic Jew: a member of a Jewish mystic movement founded in the eighteenth century in eastern Europe by Baal Shem Tov that reacted against Talmudic learning and maintained that God's presence was in all of one's surroundings and that one should serve God in one's every deed and word.

mitzvah. Izzy felt it was his decision to make; it no longer belonged to his parents. After all, he now had the same rights as a full-grown man.

As he'd left the apartment the night of his bar mitzvah, many years before, he'd heard the last words his father would say to him: "You're dead to me!"

Michael went to the bank the day they returned with the oranges with nine hundred dollars, equal to a more than a full year's pay working for Nicholas Cappelli. He was on his way, and he knew how to get there. The sky was the limit after such a profitable day. All Michael could hear in his mind was *Work smarter, work harder, and work longer.*

Michael and Izzy went to celebrate that night. They headed to Grace Bar and Grill down on Fifteenth Street located in the lobby of New York's Fitch Hotel. Part of Grace Bar and Grill housed prostitutes, and part contained a large, upper-class gambling den. Secret doors led to private rooms where the girls lived and worked under the watchful eye of the owner and madam, Anna Charme[2] who was a beautiful blond German woman with perfect tits.

Her establishment was frequented by the police chiefs, judges, and local and Washington politicians when in town. Madame Charme became very wealthy from her business. It enabled her to have her own car and driver. Her home was paid for in cash, by one of her clients who had to leave the country. Not only was Michael there for the whores, but he was also there to make contacts. He was introduced to this mecca by Anthony Giuseppe, who later became the Democratic city alderman.[3] He would also later become known as Tony the Butcher.

All the chatter at the bar in between sips of, whiskey, and beer was about who made what arrest, how the judge would sentence some piece-of-shit criminal, and who would win the next election.

Michael was quite at home in this environment and loved the whores as much as Izzy loved them.

---

2 A German name, pronounced Char-may, meaning charm and grace, thus Grace Bar and Grill.

3 An alderman is a member of a municipal or council in many jurisdictions founded upon old English law and is a high-ranking member of a borough or county council, a council member chosen by the elected members themselves rather than by popular vote or a council member elected by voters.

CHAPTER 8

M.P. PRODUCE EXPEDITORS was growing fast. Michael was adding new customers every day. Good money and a very good business helped Michael accumulate a list of valuable contacts—not to mention information from all his visits to Grace Bar and Grill.

The prostitutes loved the business relationships they had with Michael. They were able to see for themselves how things were lining up for this handsome young man with a bright future. In the backs of their minds, they thought that maybe, somehow, Michael could benefit their futures also. God only knew.

The going rate for a prostitute from Madame Charme was between two and three dollars. Most of the time, Michael would leave a twenty-dollar bill on the bureau. Michael always tipped well both for the sex and for information.

"Listen, baby, besides those beautiful legs, keep those ears open, and there's plenty more where this came from."

The hooker answered, "Most definitely. You know you are my favorite."

The hookers had a special way of making their customers talk about things they normally did not talk about to others, even their wives.

Sitting at the bar having a cocktail, you could hear the chatter of customers before and after their visits with the staff.

"Painted ladies of the night really make you feel all right," sang the bartender. Half a dozen heads nodded in agreement, not giving a second thought to the bits and pieces of information that rolled off their tongues.

Michael never minded leaving additional money for the bits and pieces of information he received. This information had the potential of one day helping him catapult to the top of the mountain he was climbing using his mantra,

"Work smarter, harder, and longer" than anyone else.

CHAPTER 9

THE YEARS WERE steamrolling by as fast as the new streets were being paved and tarred. A person's nose would swell with the awful odor of coal tar creosol.

The new streets were like clockwork during the summer months. Starting with the summer of 1918, the new Daylight Saving Time law was put into effect, and the long summer days lasted until eight o'clock in the evening.

The long summer days and coal tar creosol paving machines were as relentless as two rams butting heads to establish dominance.

The road machines wanted dominance as they rolled right into the 1920s.

This was progress in America.

CHAPTER 10

AT A DEMOCRATIC fund-raising event for an upcoming election in the Bronx, Old Man Cappelli invited Michael to Sunday dinner with the family.

Although Michael had not seen Mama Cappelli and their daughters since leaving Cappelli and Sons, he could still smell the summer-flower toilet water that Regina wore. Michael hoped she would remember their conversation when she'd whispered to him, "I'm glad you're not my brother."

Now he whispered to himself over and over those exact words: "I'm glad you're not my brother. I'm glad you're not my brother. I'm glad you're not my brother."

Sunday, June 6, 1920, could not arrive soon enough.

CHAPTER 11

THE SPECIAL SUNDAY finally arrived. Michael had on a new tie, a freshly laundered white shirt, and two cigars in his suit coat pocket. Nervously knocking on the door, his nostrils expanded when he caught the aroma of Mama Cappelli's homemade spaghetti sauce wafting through the hallway. In that instant, he realized how he'd missed the family setting, his parents, his uncle, and the farm back in Italy.

Regina's heart was beating faster than usual as she scurried to open the door while fussing with her hair and straightening her summer dress. She cried out, "*Vado a prendere la porta,*" anticipating Michael's presense. As the door opened, he stared at a beautiful woman with radiant skin; long, dancer's legs; and a smile to warm the coldest of hearts. It was Regina Cappelli, the eldest daughter.

"Regina, I'm—I'm—glad… I haven't seen you for so long."

"Almost five years," Regina quickly replied. "*Venir dentro.* Come in, come in. I'll call Papa."

Mama Cappelli came running to greet Michael. "*Ah, bellissimo ragazzo,*" she said as she gave him a hug and kissed him on both cheeks. Regina's sisters, Theresa and Maria, could be heard giggling from the kitchen.

Old Man Cappelli was coming up the stairs from the basement holding a gallon of red wine he'd made about a year ago. "*Ah, Michael, e bello vedere che si.*"

"It's good to see you too, Mr. Cappelli."

He turned his attention to his daughter. "Regina, get us some glasses and help your mother." Mr. Cappelli poured out wine as the two spoke about business and how Michael was sorely missed in the store. What Mr. Cappelli didn't say was how happy he was to see how successful Michael had become, especially because of Michael's interest in Regina. He wanted to be sure of Michael's intentions. Mr. Cappelli was not ignorant knowing well what Michael's intentions were with Regina. . After all, he had been young himself and remembered how he'd looked at Mrs. Cappelli back then.

Chapter 12

As they sat at the dinner table, Michael relished every bit of attention he was getting, especially from Regina. Her beautiful, soft brown eyes complemented the natural highlights of her hair and olive skin. Each word she spoke was like the fragrance of freshly cut flowers that would roll through the air as the breeze of the day passed. Everyone was catering to Michael as if he were the one-eyed prince living right in the middle in the land of the blind.

Michael soon directed the dinner conversation to center on the Cappelli business, home, and family. He had a natural ability to disarm people and have them feel as though they were the center of the universe. These natural skills had been honed in his daily business and also during the education he gleaned at Grace Bar and Grill. The Cappellis were captivated by Michael's ways.

Old Man Cappelli lifted the wine jug only to realize it was empty, and he excused himself to retrieve another bottle of red from the basement. Upon his return to the table, Regina said, "Papa, Michael asked me to walk along South Street."

"Only with your permission, Mr. Cappelli," Michael added quickly as Cappelli poured more wine. Mama Cappelli was tense while Theresa and Maria whispered to each other behind their napkins.

"What's in your pocket?" asked the old man.

"Ah! Fresh Havanas for you," said Michael as he handed them to the head of the house. As Cappelli accepted, he ran his nose across the long, tightly wrapped cigars. He reached in his pocket and displayed a beautiful silver cigar cutter shaped like a bullet. He cut into the cigar to make a perfect round hole, struck a match, and started puffing.

"Be home by eight thirty," he answered.

Both old man Cappelli and Michael lifted their glasses to each other, saying, "*Per mille anni*"[1] before sipping more wine.

---

1 For a thousand years.

CHAPTER 13

AN ITALIAN TRADITION was that Sunday dinner began at two o'clock. Michael was becoming a regular guest at the Cappellis on Sundays. The menu always included pasta, meatballs, wine, espresso, and *savoiardi* cookies. Old Man Cappelli would have to loosen his belt to enjoy the fruits of his labor since he provided everything that was set out on the dining room table.

Each visit led to Michael becoming more familiar with the family. There were many stories of the Italy left behind, the sagas of people—relatives, friends, neighbors—and their difficult times and their good times. As these stories were told, eyebrows would raise, hands would wave about, and smiles would come and go. Eyes would swell with emotion, both joy and sorrow. Some of the stories were repeated over and over again and probably would continue to be passed down, generation to generation. This was Sunday, every Sunday.

Everyone looked forward to Sunday all week.

Michael and Regina were falling in love. It was a natural love, not forced or prearranged as back in the Old Country. Mr. and Mrs. Cappelli felt that love should not be forced. They were not in the Old Country. Mr. and Mrs. Cappelli had fallen in love in the New World, and their three children had been born in the New World, America.

They wanted the New World ways for Regina, Maria, and Theresa.

CHAPTER 14

EVERY MOMENT REGINA could escape to be with Michael, she would. Her two younger sisters would help by asking their parents for permission to go out with Regina.

"Can we go to church and say the evening novena?"[1] "Can we go to church to say the Stations of the Cross?"[2] Mama and Old Man Cappelli loved that their daughters were so close and all had such godly devotion. For Mama, Sunday Mass was enough devotion for her. Nicholas Cappelli was certain that the closeness they had for one another and their shared closeness to God was an added protection for his three beautiful girls. Once out of the house, Theresa and Maria would go walking down the avenue window-shopping, and Regina would go to Michael's office on South Street. However, instead of going into the office door, Regina would take a few steps down the side street to the door that was the entrance to Michael's apartment.

Here is where Regina surrendered her virginity to Michael. Here is where Michael surrendered his soul to Regina. Even though Michael had been with countless women sexually, he had never been with a woman he loved before. The tenderness, the longing, the lust had never been as satisfying as this. Regina was completely bewitched by Michael's sexual abilities. She surrendered willingly and eagerly, and she enjoyed the need to have Michael touch the once-hidden

---

1   A novena (from Latin: *Novem, meaning Nine*) is an institutional act of religious pious devotion in the Roman Catholic Church often consisting of private or public prayers repeated for nine successive days in belief of obtaining special intercessory graces.

2   The object of the Stations of the Cross is to help the faithful make a spiritual pilgrimage of prayer, through meditating upon the chief scenes located on the inner walls of the church, depicting Christ's sufferings and death.

places on her perfect body. When both collapsed in total fulfillment from their lovemaking, they were as one, bonded together.

These rendezvous were becoming as regular as possible. Regina looked for every opportunity to slip away without raising Mama's and Papa Cappelli's suspicion. If they found out Regina and Michael were having premarital sex, they would be crushed by their betrayal of Italian tradition. It would be unforgivable, even though they had probably done it themselves before they were married. After all, the lure of sex had been around since Adam and Eve.

"You have to try the shoes on to be sure they fit and you can walk in them" were the words of advice from the whores at Grace Bar and Grill to any customer thinking of marriage.

It never seemed out of place that prostitutes were encouraging their clients to get to know their future wives sexually. They said this many times to Michael, but he never associated their advice with Regina. He already knew she was the perfect fit for him, and he would walk anywhere for her and with her.

Grace Bar and Grill continued to be a frequent haunt, but now it was more for the opportunity to grow his power by associating with the contacts he was making.

CHAPTER 15

WITHIN A YEAR Michael and Regina were married. The wedding ceremony was held at Our Lady of Fatima Church on 187th Street in the Bronx. It was open to anyone who wanted to attend, and the church became very crowded very quickly.

Michael's contacts were spread far and wide. Most of his business associates attended. Most of his contacts from Grace Bar and Grill attended, and when word got out that the bishop would perform the wedding ceremony—a privilege only for very special people and dignitaries—not one seat was available. The bishop performed the marriage ceremony as a favor owed to Michael from the church.

Regina felt a special aura as she walked down the aisle, her father by her side. He was so proud of both Regina and Michael knowing Regina would be well cared for the rest of her life.

Theresa and Maria were Regina's bridesmaids. They wore soft green silk dresses. Mama Cappelli chose a lavender gown to represent purple, the color for royalty. Izzy, Michael's best man, wore a tuxedo similar to the one Michael wore.

Their wedding reception, by invitation only, was warm, friendly, and, of course, Italian. The reception was held at the Chaetae on Houston Street, downtown Manhattan. Family and friends ate, danced, and drank just as they would have done back in Italy. Although some distant relatives were in attendance, Michael missed his parents, knowing they would have been so happy to be at his wedding and meet his precious Regina.

But Michael had to keep his focus and his mantra, "Work smarter, harder, and longer." That's why his contacts and friends were growing as he'd planned. He was aware that who you knew was just as important as what you knew. Favors came to Michael as easy as the tide came in at the East River basin.

As Regina looked around at the 379 people in attendance, she couldn't help but wonder how Michael knew the police chief, a city councilman, judges, and the assistant district attorney, as well as some other politicians from Brooklyn, the Bronx, and Lower Manhattan.

Ah, the Grace Bar and Grill!

CHAPTER 16

THE THREE-LAYER WEDDING cake was a gift to Michael and Regina. The favors were also a gift. The favors were given to the wedding guests from the bride and groom as a thank-you for coming and as a reminder of Michael and Regina's wedding. These gifts were from Michael's contacts who wanted to get to know him and be associated with him. They saw something in Michael that just emanated huge success, pending wealth, and important contacts that people would kill to have. They had no idea how true that would ring in the near future. They were a mix of *paesans*, Irish, and of course, the Jews, who all wanted to be part of Michael's life and future.

Recalling his days at temple, Izzy always told Michael, "All these people are like those found in the book of Zechariah... In those days, ten men would take hold, out of all the languages of the nations; they would take hold of the skirt of him who is a Jew, saying, 'We will go with you, for we have heard that God is with you.'"

They certainly knew Michael wasn't a Jew, and there was no proof that God was with him. Something was with Michael though, and those who followed him really didn't give a shit what "it" was. They knew there were many different people who were going to be with him, including the Jews, Italians, Irish, judges, politicians, police chiefs, whores, and business owners. So why not take hold of his figurative skirt too?

Michael didn't care about other people's heritage or religious beliefs. Relion was there for anyone who wanted to use it for whatever reason they saw fit, even as a bargaining tool.

"It's all bullshit," he would say. That's one reason he and Izzy got along so well.

He found the church was just as corrupt as the politicians. As a matter of fact, the bishop who performed the wedding ceremony carried a gun. One day, as the bishop was preparing for a local politician's High Mass funeral, someone saw the gun in the sacristy, the room where priests would get ready for mass.

Even though no one knew where he'd gotten the gun, no one ever questioned it. Michael didn't have to question it because Michael knew. Michael was the one the bishop asked to get him a gun. Michael didn't care about all the bullshit of traditions and ceremonies. What he cared about was: How will these people get me where I'm going, and how fast can I get there?

The bishop returned the favor to Michael. He understood that Michael didn't care about traditions and ceremonies, but Michael cared about Regina's happiness when the bishop performed the wedding ceremony. It was fitting because she attended Mass every Sunday with her mother and two sisters. What the bishop didn't know was that Regina was having great sex with Michael before marriage. Regina felt being so in love was all that mattered, and that God knew that. Now she would be married while having great sex, and God knew that too!

CHAPTER 17

MICHAEL AND REGINA took off for their honeymoon a few days later. He reviewed things with Izzy, since Izzy was the only one Michael trusted to be in charge of business while Michael was away.

"Regina, I know you'll love Florida. It has sunshine all the time, beautiful blue skies, warm water, and miles of beaches. I fell in love with Florida on my very first trip with Izzy, when we bought oranges to begin the business."

"We'll see, Michael. We shall see."

The plane took off from Teterboro Airport. This was the first time flying for both of them.

"Michael, I have to pray. I'm going to say the rosary. I'm a little nervous about this flying stuff."

"Go ahead. I'll be quiet." Their plane landed a few hours later at Wilcox Field Miami, Florida.

Michael and Regina were met by a man dressed in a dark suit, tie, and hat, even though it was a balmy eighty degrees. He nodded and bowed slightly as he said, "Michael, ma'am, New York City Councilman Roberts sent me to pick you both up. I'll be your driver. My name is Dominick Corsico. I'd prefer if you call me Fats. Welcome to Florida, the Sunshine State."

"Thanks, Fats," Michael said. "I've been here before—sort of got my start here."

"I heard that. Glad you're considering doing some business here."

"When were you going to tell me?" Regina whispered to Michael.

Michael leaned in close to Regina's ear. "I've made some important contacts here through Anthony Guiseppe. He was at our wedding. You met him. It's going to be great for business. Shh…later." As a distraction, Michael pointed out the window. "Look at that water. Isn't it beautiful? Fats, will you be available if I need to contact you?"

"Sure, Michael. Just call me. I'll write my office number for you. Here we are at the beautiful Flamingo Hotel. It's practically brand-new. It's only been opened a few years. That's Biscayne Bay on that side and the Atlantic Ocean on the other side. I'm here if you need anything. Here's a telephone number. Enjoy your stay."

Fats took the luggage out of the trunk, tipped his hat, said, "Ma'am," and got back in the car and drove away. The bellhop ran out to get the bags.

CHAPTER 18

THERE WASN'T ANYTHING that either Michael or Regina wanted from Fats. What they wanted was sex and lots of it. There was no hesitation. Once they reached the room, Michael got rid of the bellboy with a two-dollar tip, and they tumbled onto the bed.

Just as a young child stands in front of a display case in a bakery, with eyes only for the chocolate cake with chocolate icing in front of them, Michael and Regina saw only each other.

Slowly their clothes fell to the floor, piece by piece, kiss by kiss. The chiffon curtains blew into the room as skin meshed with skin, and their bodies glistened in the afternoon heat. As their temperatures rose, they greedily indulged in each other, and the bed became their stage. As Michael's mouth found Regina's nipples, she moved on top of Michael, kissing him as she was filled with his manhood. Regina's scent was like summer honeysuckle, and its sweetness caused him to immediately release control to her. Michael matched her rhythm, and both were able to pump as smoothly as a locomotive engine pumping steam. They moaned in ecstasy as they surrendered to each others embrace.

"Don't stop," Michael whispered. Still hot and burning, Michael welcomed the collapsed weight of Regina. "I love you."

"I love you more," Regina said. Both totally spent, they lay naked on the bed as the balmy ocean breeze lulled them to sleep.

CHAPTER 19

OVER THE NEXT few days, they never left the hotel room. They lived the honeymooners dream: sex and more sex. They had casual sex and intense sex and lustful lovemaking. In between, they slept, showered, and ate food but not necessarily in that order. All these components were constant as they reached their record of seven times in one day.

When the telephone rang, Michael picked up the receiver.

"Hello."

"Michael, this is Fats. Mayor Spencer and his wife would like to take you and Mrs. Pellegrino to dinner. I'll pick you up at five p.m. He likes to dine early. Be outside."

Click.

"Regina, we have a dinner invitation from the mayor of Miami and his wife, and we'll be picked up at five. C'mon, we have time for one more."

Regina could not stop thinking about the invitation and could not concentrate on Michael's efforts. As soon as they finished, Regina asked, "How did we get invited to dinner by the mayor and his wife?"

"That's what you were thinking of while I was pouring my heart out to you?" Michael said.

"Yeah, pouring your heart out to me and pouring yourself into me," replied Regina.

"I was able to contact him through the Bronx Coalition. He wants to reach out to us to bring business to Miami."

"Reach out to us how?" asked Regina.

Michael chose his reply to Regina carefully. "He's a businessman. I'm a businessman. I can deliver products and services cheaper to Miami than anyone else. It's that simple. We have a lot to offer, and he knows it."

"What's in it for him?" Regina questioned.

"There's always something in it for someone," answered Michael. He wasn't telling Regina the entire truth though.

"OK, I'll start to get ready."

At five o'clock sharp, Michael and Regina stepped outside the lobby. They both were dressed so elegantly, they looked like fashion models. The car was parked under the canopy, and Fats was standing by the car door.

"Good evening, Michael, Mrs." Fats opened the car door for them.

"Michael, what does Fats do?" Regina whispered.

Michael shrugged his shoulders. "He's the mayor's driver, I guess." Michael knew he wasn't just the driver. He knew exactly what Fats did. Some things Regina just didn't need to know.

CHAPTER 20

THE CONVERSATION FLOWED very easily as everyone was getting to know one another. After a thorough exchange of small talk, about an hour into dinner, Mayor Spencer said he wanted to talk about more serious matters.

"Michael, you should consider shortening your name, say, to Pell. It's good for business. People judge you by a lot of different things, including your background and where your name comes from. Pell is nonthreatening, easy to remember, and has strength. My family name was Spensinsky. Now it's Spencer, Mayor Spencer. Do you think I would have become mayor of Miami with a name like Spensinsky and coming from Philadelphia?

"Florida is going to be an up-and-coming state for growth, tourists, and maybe one day, legal gambling. Cuba's only ninety miles from Miami. It's becoming a playground destination, with casinos in Havana. They're going to need hotels and, more importantly, people who know how to run things the right way when it comes to booze, food, and gambling. And Cuba's President Zepeda wants to modernize his country. Mr. Pell, we're talking millions of dollars in our pockets."

Michael thought, *and prostitutes.* He knew the mayor wouldn't say "prostitutes" in front of their wives. He left this important component out as a courtesy, but Michael knew it was part of the "booze, food, and gambling."

On the plane ride home, Regina talked nonstop. "I think Mayor Spencer has a good idea about changing our name. We'll be Americanized. I see his point about not being attached to any group of people that some people may not want to do business with. I believe he's right about Florida and Cuba. Can you imagine business in another country? I want you to succeed. I want us to succeed. I'm willing to stand with you if you decide to change names and bring whatever you have to Florida and Cuba. It doesn't mean you will leave behind your memories or what your name has stood for. I've changed my name to yours. We'll have future memories with a future name. It sounds nice, real nice—Michael and Regina Pell. It has a nice flow to it. I love you, Mr. Pell." Then she continued her rosary. "Hail Mary full of Grace..."

Michael's thoughts were running nonstop: the future, their future, with a different name? Regina liked the idea of this whole new change? Florida, Cuba, booze, food, gambling, and prostitutes.

He wondered what would be harder—to actually change or to accept change.

Michael kept thinking about Mayor Spencer's suggestion.

CHAPTER 21

UPON RETURNING HOME to New York, Michael wasn't surprised to find that Izzy had taken care of business in the usual fashion.

"No problems; only solutions," as Izzy would always say.

CHAPTER 22

M.P. PRODUCE EXPEDITORS continued to expand. The business was growing and so was the staff. Michael hired sales help, office staff, and more deliverymen. The most important new hire was someone to collect money due. Michael was lending money and getting a very high rate of interest in return. The people borrowing the money usually couldn't get a conventional loan from a bank. Sometimes the borrowers wanted to open their own business, or they had to pay for a funeral or a wedding. Michael didn't care why they wanted the money or how they used the money. They knew they weren't going to get the money anywhere else, and they were willing to pay for it. Michael just cared that they paid back the principal and the *vig,* or the interest, in the time period set out. A borrower not meeting this obligation could cost Michael more than lost principal and interest. It could send the message to other borrowers that they didn't have to pay Michael back. If a borrower took that risk, Michael would have to send his own message. In the beginning, some took that chance. They lost.

A Brooklyn attorney borrowed money from Michael. He was introduced to Michael by Izzy. Somehow he felt he was better than some money lending punk and was not repaying the loan or the *vig.* Izzy's solution was to send Anthony Giuseppe, who would offer the attorney an option. This is how Anthony Giuseppe got the nickname, Tony the Butcher.

Anthony Giuseppe was not a large man but could be very persuasive and intimidating. His right eye always looked to the far right. However, when he opened his eyes wide, it would bulge as if it were going to pop out of his head. When he did this, he looked like a crazy person and sent children running. The story his aunt told him was that it was due to a trauma when he was a baby. His mother abandoned him in the hospital, where he was mistreated and possibly fell on his head.

Neatly dressed in suit, tie, and hat, Anthony looked like an attorney himself. He entered the Brooklyn office, tipped his hat to the receptionist in the front room, and walked right into the private office and closed the door behind him. The attorney sitting at his desk was caught off guard. As he was standing up, Anthony grabbed the attorney's arm twisting it, causing the attorney to fall to the floor breaking his glasses, gasping for breath as he stared at this stranger with a bulging eye.

Anthony spoke softly through gritted teeth. "You're so fucking far behind on your loan to Michael. Now you owe double *vig*. You have two days for the money—all the money! If not, your family will identify you with a meat cleaver sticking out of your fucking head. A man such as yourself realizes there's no security to protect you when you don't pay what you owe."

Mr. Giuseppe turned, walked through the door, tipped his hat to the receptionist one more time, and left the office.

The money was paid in full, and Anthony Giuseppe got his nickname, Tony the Butcher.

Chapter 23

THEN THERE WAS the time a body was found floating in the Harlem River basin by the rowing team from Columbia University. It was the body of the mayoral candidate for Yonkers, John Forgerty. In his place, Bert Cunningham was elected, unopposed. One of the first people to congratulate Bert was his friend Mayor Bob Spencer of Miami.

Michael was reaping the benefits of his contacts. There was an abundance of favors owed to him stemming from his contacts from the Grace Bar and Grill, and they continued to flow in, one way or another.

Anthony Giuseppe, aka Tony the Butcher, would often drive his big blue Buick, a gift from Michael, to the Harlem River Park on his way home. It was one of his favorite spots to enjoy the sights and smells of the river. Once in a while, he'd bring a woman to this place to drink whiskey and indulge in the big backseat of his big blue Buick. He parked along the side of a wall, making it impossible to see his car, yet there was a perfect view of the river, the lights, and whatever else might be happening.

CHAPTER 24

MICHAEL AND REGINA returned from their honeymoon to the small apartment behind the South Street office. Due to his growing businesses, Michael decided it was time to open a second office in the Bronx, and he and Regina would live there as well. Regina proved to be extremely valuable, as she helped make these changes. She certainly was not afraid of change. She spoke with Michael about changing their name to Pell, as the mayor of Miami had suggested. Michael was reluctant and worried about traditions.

"They'll always be there, Michael, and we'll make new traditions and new memories," insisted Regina.

Michael didn't realize it would be so easy. Soon, after visiting some of his contacts at the courthouse, it was done. It was as simple as saying, "God bless you," after someone sneezed.

Regina sent a telegram to Mayor Spencer and his wife:

Dear Bob and Virginia, STOP

Thank you for your hospitality and friendship. STOP

We have seriously considered putting into motion what you suggested.

STOP

We would like to extend an open invitation to you both whenever you may be in New York. STOP

Sincerely, STOP
Michael and Regina Pell STOP

CHAPTER 25

M.P. PRODUCE EXPEDITORS and Michael's moneylending were expanding from Little Italy in Lower Manhattan to New York's other boroughs, including the Bronx, parts of Brooklyn, and to upstate New York, near the Saratoga race-track. Michael recognized people needed money to gamble. As a kid with his shoeshine box, Michael had told his customers, "Stay one step ahead of the shoe-shine." Now he was applying this to himself and his growing business. He would take the next logical step and open gambling parlors and combine moneylend-ing, so people could bet on horse racing. He remembered his meeting with Mayor Spencer of Miami and their conversation about expanding to Florida. If he could expand to Florida, what about all the states in between?

M.P. Produce Expeditors rented a new office at the corner of Third and Tremont Avenue. It was twice the size of the office on South Street. Regina found a beautiful apartment nearby on Hoffman Street, directly across from a row of small, family-owned businesses. The apartment, located on the second floor, had two bedrooms and one bathroom, and it was in excellent condition. Everything worked well, including the pull chain overhead to flush the toilet box. The superintendent of the building was a man called Whitey. Whitey, nicknamed for his extremely white hair, was an all-around guy who could fix anything and gambled on everything. As the story goes, he once bet on two roaches crawling up a wall to see which one would reach the ceiling first.

Many things were changing throughout the country, from neighborhoods, to people and politics. Prominent groups such as the Woman's Christian Temperance Union and the Anti-Saloon League were urging the states and Congress to pass a constitutional amendment that would ban the manufacture, sale, and transportation of alcohol. In this instance, the US Constitution was not changed to radically restrict the personal liberties of the people—that is, it wasn't done at that time.

CHAPTER 26

MANY DIVERSE CULTURES settled in the Bronx, including Irish, German, Jewish, and Italian immigrants. These residents helped build the Bronx.

Fordham University owned the land, which became the Bronx Zoo and New York Botanical Garden. Fordham University sold it to the city of New York for $1,000 under the condition that the lands be used for a zoo and garden in order to create a natural buffer between the university grounds and the urban expansion that was nearing. In the 1880s, New York State set aside the land for future development as parks. In 1895, New York State chartered the New York Zoological Society for the purpose of founding a zoo. The zoo was originally named the Bronx Zoological Park and the Bronx Zoological Gardens. It opened its doors to the public on November 8, 1899, housing 843 animals on 265 acres.

Arthur Avenue was the commercial center of this Fordham section of the Bronx known as Little Italy. Each borough housed its own ethnic sections, whether Italian, Irish, Jewish, or Polish. The avenue was lined with store after store filled with vegetables, sausages, hanging beef, homemade pastas, cheeses, and Italian pastries. It was Mayor Fiorello LaGuardia who spearheaded the Arthur Avenue Retail Market, which housed a variety of vendors under one roof. The pushcarts lined the curbs and came in every shape and size, selling a wide assortment of products, including nuts, fish, and assorted Italian delights. The smoke and the smell of the chestnuts would fill the surrounding area and entice one to buy a bag or two. If you wanted to operate a pushcart on the street, you had to be approved by the neighborhood coalition, which consisted of a group of men who called the shots; there was a pecking order for you to get approval.

Michael originated the neighborhood coalition, thanks to and with the help of his contacts at Grace Bar and Grill. The approved vendors would have to kick in to the coalition, which in turn divvied up the money. No one could just add a pushcart without the coalition's permission. There was a brazen, thickheaded Calabrese woman who thought she could put a second cart on the street because she was already paying for a spot on a busy corner. She and her second pushcart were run down by a big blue car. There weren't any eyewitnesses, except for the victim, who could only remember the color of the car, so the police didn't have a description of the driver. The second pushcart was destroyed, and the woman barely survived the hit and run. Due to her injuries, she had to wear a special shoe with a two-inch sole because her damaged leg was now shorter than the other. When questioned by the police, she had some memory loss about what had happened. She couldn't remember anything, just the color blue. The cops believed her memory loss was part of a head injury. Case closed!

Around the corner on Hughes Avenue and 186th Street was the Savoy Theatre, which later became known as Cinell's Italian-American Savoy. On special nights, the Savoy would not show a movie. Instead, there would be an opera or a live play by traveling Italian actors. These were special to the neighborhood residents and brought memories of the land and families they'd left behind but still carried in their hearts.

On Decatur Avenue was Edison Manufacturing Company, a movie studio run by director Edwin S. Porter and owned by Thomas Edison. There was another studio on 176th Street where silent films were produced.

Michael often heard "the future is the Bronx," and needless to say, both Michael and Regina were right in the middle of it all in order to be *one step ahead of the shoeshine* as he told his shoe shine customers as a kid shining shoes.

CHAPTER 27

ON MARCH 21, 1922, almost nine months from the day of their wedding, Regina gave birth to a son, eight pounds, eight ounces. Michael always believed in how numbers worked, and eight pounds, eight ounces was great because they were not only the same number, but they also were even numbers and considered very lucky.

He knew the formula for the birth date March 21, 1922.

2+1 for the day equals 3.
1+9+2+2 for the year equals 14; then 1+4 equals 5.
3+5 equals another 8.

Michael believed good fortune would be in this baby's life, regardless that Charles was born breech. Because of the complications with the breech, Regina would not be able to have any additional children.

At one time, both Regina and Michael had thought the baby's middle name would be Isaiah, after Izzy. However, as Americanized as the Pells were becoming, tradition for the Pellegrino and Cappelli family history won out. Charles was Michael's father's name, and Nicholas was Regina's father's name, so their son's name would be Charles Nicholas Pell.

Michael reflected back on the day he'd arrived on Ellis Island sixteen years ago, knowing he would have respect for himself and his family. He wished his mother and father were there to share in the magical moment of their grandson's birth.

His plans were growing stronger and faster than even he had planned. He was proud and had to continue his mantra even more—work smarter, harder, and longer.

Family and friends gathered at Fordham Hospital the next day to greet new baby Charles. Old Man Cappelli was crying, saying with his thick accent, "Look, look at that beautiful boy. He has my name right in the middle. Charles Nicholas Pellegrino—I mean, Charles Nicholas Pell."

Mama Cappelli as well as Theresa and Maria were crying tears of joy as they pointed through the hospital glass, saying, "*Bella*, beautiful, beautiful *bambino*. We love you!"

CHAPTER 28

THE PAGES OF the calendar were flipping as fast as you could flip a steak. The Bronx was becoming more popular with each turn of the page. Many restaurants, storefronts, and offices were opening. Along with them were illegal gambling rooms, which brought out the local coalition to organize and keep things running smoothly.

The area had become a mecca for living and playing, influenced by new businesses and the electricity that was permeating the air. On Kingsbridge Road off Fordham Road, there was an ice-cream parlor with small black-and-white square floor tiles, wooden chairs, and marble tables. It was a neighborhood favorite, with great ice cream, including a dish called the Kitchen Sink. It was large enough to serve six to eight people. During the summer months, you would have to wait in line to get a seat.

Up the street was Poe Park. It was a nice park with the old cottage where Edgar Allan Poe, had lived with his wife, Virginia, and her mother, Mrs. Clemm. They moved from Midtown Manhattan to what was then the little Village of Fordham in a desperate attempt to reverse Virginia's declining health. She had contracted tuberculosis some years earlier, the same as Michael's mother had. Sadly, the attempt proved futile, and Virginia passed away in the cottage on January 30, 1847.

The Bronx was a beautiful place. Michael, Regina, and Charles would visit Poe Park after their Sunday ice cream. Michael would mingle and consort with many of the neighborhood business owners.

Michael and his family never had to wait in line anywhere for anything, even outside the confines of the Bronx. His reputation as the leader of the Bronx

Coalition preceded him wherever he went. For many he was better known as belonging to the *guapparia,* a word in the Neapolitan language to indicate a member of the Mafia type organization in the region of Campania and its capital, Naples.

CHAPTER 29

THE UNITED STATES of America was trying to find itself and to better its 106 million residents.

Drastic change rolled in with drastic moneymaking opportunities. The Eighteenth Amendment (Amendment XVIII) of the US Constitution established the prohibition of alcoholic beverages in the United States. The separate Volstead Act (named after Andrew Volstead, a member of the a US House of Representatives) set down methods of enforcing the Eighteenth Amendment and defined which intoxicating liquors were prohibited and which were excluded from prohibition, for example, for medical and religious purposes. The amendment was the first to set a time delay before it would take effect following ratification and the first to set a time limit for its ratification by the states. Its ratification was certified on January 16, 1919, with the amendment taking effect on January 17, 1920.

Over the few years before this, before Regina gave birth, Michael had been a keen observer of new opportunities and analyzed what would be the right circumstances and when would be the right time to participate in this wonderful world of wealth. The Bronx Coalition, produce expediting, and moneylending were all doing very well. Michael's mantra was serving him very well.

Demand for liquor and beer continued, and the amendment resulted in the criminalization of producers, suppliers, and transporters. Consumers did not care about the law and wanted their booze. The police, courts, attorneys, and prisons were overwhelmed with new cases. Organized crime increased in power and corruption, and extended to include law enforcement officials as well as politicians. Michael didn't miss a beat. The doors of the late 1920s had swung open, and Michael was standing in the doorway to enter with a roar. Violence was on the increase. . Rival groups vied for any advantage to reap the huge amounts of money ready to be made. Michael would often repeat what he heard growing up in anticipation of coming to America, that the streets were paved with gold in America. Michael was not going to have any gold slip away, which for him meant anything that could make him more money or more powerful contacts. This type of gold was certainly in his future.

Like a spider weaves a well-organized web, Michael wove all his political and religious friends and business contacts. He identified all those he could trust and some he might not. He had a keen awareness of his enemies. Many of the religious leaders in the area would come to the local political party functions and seek out the coalition for favors for the church. The priests needed to get to know those who ran things, and they realized they would have to return the favors someday. Although the bishop would appear at some of the more public functions, he would often meet privately with Michael and some coalition members for certain favors.

CHAPTER 30

REGINA KEPT BUSY with little Charles, who was called Charlie. There was plenty of help from Mama Cappelli and Regina's sisters. They would take turns leaving the store and being away from Old Man Cappelli. While they enjoyed seeing Regina and Michael, they loved being with Charlie. Often they would stay for a few days. Regina always welcomed their company, their help, and especially their sweet love for Charlie. Mama Cappelli would cook up a storm, making her famous pasta, gravy, and meatballs. The Cappelli women would always come with loaded shopping bags filled with tomatoes, prosciutto, stuffed pork braciole, sausage, bread, cheese, and homemade red wine from Old Man Cappelli's basement. They would take the train to Tremont Avenue station, and then take a Checker Taxi the rest of the way to Hoffman Street.

The two flights of stairs wore out Mama Cappelli every time. She'd get in the apartment and hold and fuss over "baby Charles," as Mama still called him. In the meantime, the girls would put all the groceries away until the next production that was the family cooking and eating together. Mama would say, "Put the baby here, so he can watch when we cook and I sing to him."

Michael was also keeping busy with M.P. Produce Expeditors, moneylending, and now, his new business, providing beer and whiskey to anyone, from New York to Florida, who was willing to pay the price for it.

Mayor Spencer called Michael about going to Cuba for a meeting with some officials.

"I would like to cement this deal with Cuba, Mr. Pell. When can you fly there to meet me?"

Michael thought, *it's true; the streets are paved with gold. Maybe Cuba's streets are paved with gold too.*

CHAPTER 31

IT WAS TIME.

Michael knew an ex-boxer named Joey Adams. Joey located a warehouse up in Yonkers that would be used as a base for the new brewery business.

Joey used the alias Adams, as a fighter because he lived on Adams Place, which was right off Arthur Avenue. His real name was Joseph Vani. Although the Adams name stayed with him to his friends, it did not with his family. To them, he was always JoJo.

Joey was a pretty good fighter and had won many fights. Unfortunately, Joey hated to train. He would stay out all night drinking, playing cards with his friends, and partying with as many of the whores as possible from Grace Bar and Grill.

Eventually, Joey was a contender for the heavyweight championship title in 1923. But his opportunity came to an end when he fought a big guy from the United Kingdom named Mackenzie "Mac" Pharlain. By the second round, Joey was exhausted. With a left hook from his opponent, Joey hit the canvas as if he had been thrown from the roof by a gorilla. Big-time sportswriter Ray Walters described the "punch as only a smack by Mac Pharlain". So, Mac Pharlain got the nickname Smacky Mackie.

Joey Adams never fought again. He spent nine months in the hospital learning how to walk again, a complication of vertebral fractures coupled with a neuralgic deficit, causing him to walk leaning forward, creating a hunch on his back. About a year later, Smacky Mackie went on to the win the world heavyweight championship.

During Joey's recovery Michael helped by sending groceries and paying his rent and hospital bills, which Joey would never forget. He was deeply indebted to Michael Pell. Now, Joey was going to run the Yonkers warehouse. Although he lost the fight for the heavyweight championship, he still had his reputation: don't fuck with Joey Adams and don't ever mention Smacky Mackie.

Fire hoses mysteriously disappeared from firehouse station number 11 being constructed on Bronxville Road, Yonkers. They found their way to Joey for pumping beer from the huge vats into the barges.

Joey was in charge of this warehouse and chose the location in Yonkers knowing the authorities would look the other way on the say-so of Mayor Bert Cunningham.

CHAPTER 32

THE WAREHOUSE WAS along the Hudson River in downtown Yonkers, also the site of many loading docks that were once used as slaughterhouses for chickens. The rent was low because the stench could drive a spike into your nose. The location, perfect for illegal activity, was known as Chicken Island. It was now going to be used to make and transport beer and alcohol for Michael and his entourage.

Michael and his company were officially in the bootlegging[1] business to brew and transport beer and liquor across the country. M.P. Produce Expeditors was supplying restaurants and hotels from New York to Florida, so his professional ventures were tailor-made for the booze and beer business. It was the same customers, only different merchandise with different trucks.

Michael thought of it is a simple, super moneymaker. Again, his mantra kept him ahead of the competition.

He himself did not do much business with fruits and vegetables and money-lending, since he was able to have those sides of business run by those he trusted most. Why should he bother when the big money was in booze and beer, and transporting it? He was now like an orchestra conductor standing in front of many professional musicians, tapping his baton to his downbeat, telling them when to start, what to play, and when to finish. He wasn't thinking of finishing though. His downbeat had just begun.

---

1   The term bootlegging is believed to have been coined during the US Civil War, when soldiers would sneak liquor into army camps by concealing pint bottles within their boots or beneath their trouser legs.

Michael and his crew were growing their brewery business and not looking back. The music that had been playing for the past months had been quick and catchy as Michael tapped his baton. The money flowed as fast as the beer poured from the barrels. It was like hitting the sweepstakes over and over again that was always fixed in your favor.

CHAPTER 33

WHEN THE TELEPHONE rang, Michael answered. "Hello."

"Michael, this is Vince."

Vince was Michael's longtime trusted friend who oversaw the transportation of the beer barrels being shipped around the country. He had in his pocket a laundry list of important people he could call on, including politicians and police. Vince was a member of the Bronx Democratic Club and the coalition. Regardless of political preference, Vince could get it done.

"What's going on, Vince?"

"The package you ordered is going to be picked up by someone else."

"Who?"

"Kelly said the Frenchman would pick it up Friday night in Peekskill."

"Oh yes. Lieutenant Kelly," Michael said. "I remember. Thanks, Vince."

Michael hung up the phone. He knew sooner or later this had been going to happen. Bootlegging was a war among the fittest. Who could last to survive the outcome? Time would bring all things to pass. What was about to pass was the nature of survival.

In war, truth is the first casualty.

CHAPTER 34

THE FRENCHMAN WAS another bootlegger supplying a different area with beer. Lieutenant Kelly was paid handsomely by Michael for just such information, but it was always Vince who made the money drop. Lieutenant Kelly provided Vince with the information that the Frenchman was going to hijack a shipment from Michael's crew. Every route and shipment time was carefully guarded. Vince's connections were the best in this business, and their loyalty to him was better than a wife on her wedding night.

All the crazies in this business knew when someone said, "Meet you on the moon," it meant, "Meet you at the Moon Diner in Peekskill." Most drivers stopped there to grab some food and coffee on their way to or from Canada. Usually, there would be a driver and someone riding shotgun to protect the load. When they made a stop, one would run in to get food and take it back to the truck or take turns going in to use the bathroom and warm up. In other words, the truck and the load were never left unprotected. Bootleggers, also known as rumrunners, often made the trips through Canada via the Great Lakes to the Saint Lawrence Seaway and down the West Coast to San Francisco and Los Angeles just as Michael's shipments made it to the other side of the United States. He was familiar with all the routes and competition, including the Frenchman.

Michael dialed the phone. It seemed the rotor took forever to return to the original position so he could dial the next number—SE (short for Sedgwick area of the Bronx) three, 1348.

"Hello, this is Izzy."

The name Izzy in Hebrew means "God is my oath." There were many who had solid business relationships with Michael and would have done anything to protect those relationships. Izzy would do anything for Michael, anything. Izzy must have given his oath to Michael and not to God as his name indicates, because Izzy was one fucked-up, crazy Jew never neglecting that oath. The Jews and the Italians had a lot in common: family, food, and traditions.

"Izzy, Vince called. The Frenchman is going after our load this Friday."

"Where?"

"On the moon."

"You, me, and Vince will go together. Get what we'll need and be sure it will take care of everything. I want to send a message to any other motherfucker who is thinking he can hustle us. *Capito?* A big, loud, fucking message."

CHAPTER 35

FRIDAY MORNING ARRIVED quickly. Michael kissed Regina and baby Charlie and told Regina not to wait up.

"I have business in Peekskill with Izzy and Vince."

Regina understood and didn't question Michael. She knew he was a good man and he loved his family. What she didn't know was that what was going to take place in Peekskill that night would be life changing.

The day dragged by slowly, *tick, tick, tick.*

The phone rang the same as any other day. Customers called to order beer shipments, and orders were being taken to be filled. However, Michael was waiting for that special call from Izzy.

"Michael, its Izzy. Our shipment is scheduled to leave Yonkers at eight o'clock. I'm on my way to pick you up. We'll have plenty of time." Michael waited for Izzy to hang up to be sure no one was listening. When he heard the click and the dial tone, he hung up.

Michael anticipated he, Izzy, and Vince would be able to meet the truck loaded with kegs of beer and would arrive in Peekskill in plenty of time.

I've got to think this out, Michael thought.

He knew the Frenchman and knew he would have a couple of guns riding with him.

As Michael, Izzy, and Vince started their drive up to Peekskill, he tried to visualize what would take place—the neon sign for the Moon Diner, the trucks, the kegs of beer, and the Frenchman.

Izzy made sure he had brought what was needed—three shotguns, three revolvers.

About forty-five minutes into the car ride, around Croton, Izzy pulled into a Texaco gas station for some gas and to piss. As the car's front wheels rolled over the rubber hose, it rang a bell, and a second bell rang as the rear tires rolled over it.

An old man came out, wiping his hands on a dirty rag.

"Yes, sir?" the attendant said.

"Fill 'er up. Where's the shit house?" growled Izzy.

"Around the building to your right." The old man pointed.

CHAPTER 36

THEY CONTINUED UP Route 9, and they finally saw the neon sign of the Moon Diner just as the rain started to drizzle on the windshield. All three knew this had to be done quickly without hesitation.

Izzy pulled into the parking lot as the rain got heavier. All three quickly jumped out.

They saw their truck with its shipment arriving, one man riding shotgun. The driver knew Izzy, Vince, and Michael. The truck rolled to a stop, and the driver was about to get out.

Izzy told the driver to stay in the truck as he and Vince ran past, pumping the shotguns. They moved quickly toward a car with its lights on and the engine running. The two men in the car were waiting for a signal from the Frenchman to begin the heist, as their boss was sitting patiently inside the diner. He sat alone, straining to see through the rain as it ran down the window glass and clouded his view. He wanted a front row seat to give the signal and to see the heist.

It all happened within thirty seconds. To Michael, it seemed like an eternity to get inside and be face-to-face with his enemy. The truth was, this bootlegging war was about to have Michael commit his first murder.

Izzy and Vince, now running, reached the car with the Frenchman's gunmen, who were unaware of what was going on, as they drank whiskey from their flasks, laughing and joking, their windows fogging from the rain. Izzy and Vince were able to run right up to the cars with shotguns drawn, blasting as they got closer. *Blam, blam, blam, blam*—the car glass shattered, shredding the two passengers, causing a jerking, bouncing motion, and then, dead silence.

Blood continued to pour from their bodies as if it were being poured from a wide-mouth gallon jug.

Michael had made his way into the diner, pointing the revolver at the Frenchman while he tried to wipe the condensation from the window. As he saw Michael, he realized what was happening to his men and had just enough time to utter, "Jesus Christ!"

Michael fired one shot into the Frenchman's forehead that sounded like a cannon going off, echoing throughout the diner. Blood and brains splattered onto the window, the green vinyl booth, and into a piece of pie, forming a puddle of blood all over the table. The Frenchman's eyes glazed over, empty, and dead. Customers hit the floor, seeking to hide. The waitress dropped the dishes, and they smashed on the floor as she ran screaming to the kitchen.

Michael grabbed the linen napkin tucked in the dead man's shirt, wiped the gun of fingerprints, put the gun on the table, and walked out.

Michael, Izzy, and Vince got back in the car and headed home as if they had just finished having dinner.

"Too bad we didn't have time for coffee," said Izzy, laughing.

Their driver and guard drove away as fast as they could and did not stop. Michael knew that word would get out—that word would be not to fuck with Michael Pell or his business.

"We'll be home before these hick cops ever get there," Vince said.

"Kelly took care of it. He got a nice fat envelope."

"Show our appreciation, Vince. Give him another envelope. We'll get it back twofold."

"Done," Vince said.

CHAPTER 37

ON THE RIDE home, nothing more was said. The silence could not have been any thicker. The only sound was the swishing of the windshield wipers as they swept back and forth on the windshield.

The shotguns were put on the floor of the backseat, with Vince. The revolver Michael left on the table next to the Frenchman was untraceable and to be assured it would not be used in another murder.

The smell of gunpowder hung in the air, a reminder of what had just happened.

What had just happened would change lives forever.

Michael thought to himself that he now had the Frenchman's customers as part and parcel of his ungodly destruction.

Time brings all things to pass.

It was the nature of survival—the casualties of war.

Illegal war.

Bootlegging war.

M.P.'s war.

Izzy caught Michael's brazen gesture of a smile and nod of his head as if to say, 'well done'.

CHAPTER 38

EVENTUALLY, EVERYONE WOULD know Michael killed the Frenchman in addition to arranging to have many others relieved of their earthly existence.

Michael had relied on those closest and most loyal to him to do so, and he went through them one by one in his mind's eye. He listed the important loyal ones as *Izzy, Vince, Anthony Giuseppe, Joey Adams, Bert Cunningham, Lieutenant Kelly, the bishop, Dominick "Fats" Corsico, and Councilman Roberts.*

His thoughts were interrupted as he heard Regina say, "Michael, I'm glad you're home. Come to bed after you wash. I have a surprise waiting."

The stigma of committing murder can never be washed away, no matter how hard you scrub. Michael could never scrub himself clean of the darkness that lay within him as he saw his darkness in the mirror, floating in the abyss.

As he lifted his head from the sink, he said, "I'll be right there." He dried his hands and face as he stared at his reflection. He had more to accomplish on his journey regardless of how many times he washed or scrubbed.

Regina started the Victrola, carefully placing the phonograph record on the turntable and gently lowering the arm that held the needle. Now the beautiful voice of Enrico Caruso began singing the opera, *"Solo per Te,"* in his native Italian. Regina knew how much Michael loved to listen to Caruso and how much he loved to embellish the fact that Caruso came from his hometown of Naples.

She slowly turned down the sheets, running her hand across them to remove any imperfections. Slowly, she lowered herself, naked, to the bed, enjoying the song of Caruso and anticipating Michael's touch.

Solo per Te (For You Alone): English translation

Take thou this rose, this little tender rose
the rarest flower in all God's garden fair,
and let it be While yet its crimson glows
An emblem of the love I proudly, proudly bear
Take thou this heart, the heart that loves thee well
and let it flame before thy shrine, my own
Take thou my heart for oh, your dear eyes tell
God fashioned it for you, for you alone

CHAPTER 39

AFTER MANY MONTHS, arrangements were finally made to go to Cuba.

Both Regina (with rosary beads in hand) and Michael flew into Cuba via La Habana Airline, departing from New York's Roosevelt Field, named after Theodore Roosevelt's son, who was killed during World War I.

Once they landed, they were met by Fats in a car provided by Presidente Zepeda's staff.

"Hello, Fats," Regina said. "I haven't seen you since we were in Florida."

"Yes, ma'am. I'm happy to see you." He loaded the luggage. Turning, he nodded and said, "Michael."

Michael returned the simple nod and said, "I'm glad you're at the wheel, Fats. Where did you get this showboat of a car?"

"You believe it? Presidente Zepeda had a staff member drop it at the hotel. This place is quite busy—tons of people and tons of money."

"I like the sound of that," Regina said.

"Hotel En El Mar, we're here," Fats said.

"Almost the same in Italian: Hotel in the Sea," Regina said.

CHAPTER 40

HOTEL EN EL MAR was luxurious. It had four hundred rooms that catered to innumerable Ibero-American[1] heads of state, European monarchs, and top-name entertainers, crooners, and comedians.

The architecture was magnificent, with deep mahogany doors, heavy wooden ceiling beams, and inlay wood flooring that glowed with the reflections of the chandeliers, each one housing hundreds of crystal lights. The marbled lobby floors were only enhanced by the towering statues of ancient gods watching over everyone as they came and went, and sat in the silk and thick leather chairs. You could actually smell the hint of mustiness that was said to be the spirit of privateers[2] and pirates who were slaughtered in the constant attacks by the English who captured Havana. The grounds were lush with mosaic tile fountains, palm trees, and flowered paths to the beach that had private cabanas for the special guests and large cash gamblers.

---

1 Countries of South America and North America, including Central America and the islands of the Caribbean Sea south of the United States; the term is often restricted to countries where either Spanish or Portuguese is spoken. The prefix *Ibero-* refers to the Iberian Peninsula in Europe, consisting of Spain, Portugal, Andorra, and Gibraltar. Ibero-America is formed by all Spanish-speaking countries in the Americas, in addition to Brazil, which is Portuguese speaking.

2 The actual work of a *pirate* and a *privateer* is generally the same (raiding and plundering ships); it is, therefore, the authorization and perceived legality of the actions that form the distinction. At various times, governments indiscriminately granted authorization for privateering to a variety of ships, so much so that would-be pirates could easily operate under a veil of legitimacy.

Michael, Regina, and Fats were greeted by a neatly groomed elderly gentleman with snow-white hair that matched his snow-white mustache. He wore a double-breasted navy-blue uniform with ribbon medals across the left chest.

"*Saludos. Es un placer conocerlos a todos. Presidente Zepeda envía sus disculpas por su falta de comparecencia. se reunirá con nosotros más adelante.*"

The three of them, somewhat confused, stared at the man and remained speechless.

"Oh, please forgive my manners." He gently reached for Regina's hand. "Greetings. It's a pleasure to meet you all. Presidente Zepeda sends his apologies for his lack of appearance. He will meet with us later. My name is Rafael Machado, a personal assistant to Presidente Zepeda. I'm here for whatever your party may request. Let me personally show you to your rooms."

Machado snapped his fingers at the bellboy, who jumped to put all the luggage onto a cart, pushing it as fast as he could to get to the rooms before them.

"Ah, here we are," Rafael said. "I'm sure you will want to freshen up before the evening begins. Perhaps an ocean swim? Mr. Corsico, let me show you to your room."

CHAPTER 41

THE SMALL DINNER room with its arched doorways continued the hotel's elegance and charm. There were pure-white tablecloths, and the white chairs had gold sashes that matched the gold place settings.

As the guests arrived, they were met by the gracious Señor Rafael Machado. The famous Oscar Fuente Orchestra played softly in the background. Rafael guided each guest to a large round table and introduced each new arrival to those already seated. Finally, all the guests had arrived. Michael, Regina, Fats, Mayor Bob and Virginia Spencer, Florida's Senator Silver and his wife, Señor and Mrs. Rafael Machado, and Bill Sullivan, a union organizer from Chicago, and his wife, Mary.

From the outset, Sullivan faced significant challenges. Chicago's influential industrialists had outright hostility toward unions and especially about importing recruits from small Midwestern towns to become longshoremen to work loading and unloading vessels on the wharves of a port. Nevertheless, Sullivan had successfully expanded membership in the newborn union to include large numbers of dockworkers. As the union grew in size, he knew he had to add power, so he'd shifted to a main office in New York to join forces with Michael and the power Michael wielded. A lot of political bullshit had to be settled in negotiating union strikes and contracts. Michael was powerful enough to achieve this, and Bill Sullivan knew it. Michael had invited the Sullivans knowing Sullivan could be quite useful organizing the Cuban adventure.

There were many more tables filled with guests who liked to gamble. They frequented the Hotel En El Mar and were compensated for their loyalty with a variety of lavish treats.

Many of the local politicians were under the delusion that they would have a say in the Havana opportunity. In actuality, they would have as much say as the calf had about the cordon bleu veal cutlet that was being served for dinner. They were only there as trinkets, showing off their chest ribbons and medals to make the guests feel important. There were also high-class prostitutes for the men who were traveling alone. These women were undetectable as they doted on the men during an evening of dinner and dancing and more.

Eventually café Cubano was served along with Cuban pastries filled with guava and pineapple and coconut, and fresh Havana cigars for the men and cigarettes for the ladies.

Señor Machado announced that his wife would take the ladies on a special tour of the tunnels of the hotel. He explained the tunnels were once used by pirates to hide their treasure. Although the tunnels were long ago stripped of the pirate booty, perhaps the ladies would see or feel the presence of pirate spirits still seeking their spoils. In the meantime, the men would go to an informal meeting room to enjoy their café and cigars.

Señor Machado rose with a sweeping hand motion for the ladies to follow his wife.

Covering her mouth, Regina whispered to Mary, "Why are we being separated? Is it cultural, chauvinistic, or just business?" Mary didn't have an answer. She slowly raised her hands, palms out, shrugging her shoulders and giving a confused wrinkling of her eyebrows. Regina registered the emptiness of her blank stare.

Regina moved toward Michael, gently kissing him on his cheek, and whispered in his ear, "Michael, *stai attento. Non mi piace Señor Machado lui è un falso.*"[1]

---

1 Michael, be careful. I don't like Señor Machado. He is a phony.

CHAPTER 42

SEÑOR MACHADO LED the men to a room with deep oak paneling, plush carpeting, and leather chairs and couches. As Señor Machado took Michael, Fats, and Bill Sullivan on a walk, the other gentlemen were entertained. The Hotel En El Mar provided cognac, seminude Chinese women who participated in Havana's Carnival celebrations, and opium brought in from China, all at no charge.

Cuba's secretary of public health himself was a guest who indulged in both the opium and the Chinese prostitutes in spite of the fact that just a week before; he'd ordered Havana's opium addicts to be housed in one of the hospitals. Additionally, he mandated the authorities in each of Cuba's provinces to prepare a report on local Chinese associations, paying particular attention to their political and criminal activities. His report submitted to el presidente conveniently mentioned that while some of the associations devoted themselves to gambling and opium consumption, the majority were bona fide community organizations whose members were industrious and respectful of Cuba's laws. Needless to say the secretary of public health received hefty payments every month from the Chinese associations for such glowing reports.

Machado walked the three men to a private open cabana on the beach to discuss important business. Two armed army officers stood a few feet away on either side of the cabana, to assure the men inside would not be disturbed.

"Thank you for your presence," Machado began. "I have important information to share with you. El Presidente will not be present—ever! All business will be conveyed by me between you and Presidente Zepeda. I'm sure I have your confidence and support in all matters." All three men nodded in agreement. "We want Señor Bob Spencer, Miami's mayor, replaced with the vice mayor of Miami, Señor Javier Diego."

"Are you talking about Jay Dies?" Fats asked.

"That's the American name he's used for many, many years," Machado said. "It will be very worth your while, Señor Pell. All the gambling and prostitution here at the Hotel En El Mar will be under your control, along with their huge profits. The opium will be left to our government."

All three men glanced at one another as nods of approval came swiftly. They knew what Machado meant. If control of such a lucrative opportunity was going to be handed to Michael Pell on a silver platter, then Bob Spencer had to go, period. It really didn't matter why.

"This will be done in a timely matter, and you'll receive word when it's complete," said Michael as the men rose to shake Machado's hand and retreated to join the other male guests.

CHAPTER 43

WINTER 1925

BILL SULLIVAN WAS staying at the Golden Rock Hotel in Miami a few months later. As he exited the elevator on his way to enjoy a sidewalk breakfast on the magnificent, seventy-two-degree winter day, he heard quite a commotion in the lobby.

A newspaper boy was yelling, "February twenty-seventh, 1925, read all about it. Mayor Spencer and his wife killed in tragic fire."

Bill picked up a paper and generously dropped a twenty-five-cent coin on top of the stack. He read the headline word for word just as the newsboy yelled it.

"Mayor Spencer and his wife killed in tragic fire." He folded the paper, tucked it under his arm, and smirked as he walked through the revolving doors.

"Thanks a lot, mister," cried the kid, not skipping a beat, repeating, "Read all about it. Mayor Spencer and his wife killed in tragic fire."

Dominick Fats Corsico was immediately notified; he had to be at the unofficial swearing in of Jay Dies to take the mayoral position until the official ceremony could take place.

An immediate investigation was underway by Florida State Police and the state fire marshal.

CHAPTER 44

REGINA, GREATLY SADDENED, would often gasp and cry at the thought of the death of their friends, Bob and Virginia. She made arrangements to travel to Miami with Michael for their memorial service while Charlie remained with his aunts and grandmother in New York. Michael was going to have to continue on to Cuba for a meeting with Bill Sullivan and Señor Machado once the funeral services were over.

Since Mary and Bill now lived in New York, Regina and Mary Sullivan would travel back to New York together. After a few days, Mary would go to visit her family in Chicago.

Fats stayed in Miami, helping Mayor Dies ease into his new position.

Once the official swearing-in ceremony ended, Fats would be relocating to Cuba.

CHAPTER 45

As PROMISED, MICHAEL Pell was given control of the gambling and prostitution at the Hotel En El Mar. He wasted no time during his stay with Bill Sullivan to partake in all that was available to them, with the exception of opium.

The gambling rooms were quite plush with roulette, craps, blackjack, and mah-jongg. Mah-jongg, a game that originated in China, was new to the Republic of Cuba, but because of the growing number of Chinese people in Cuba, it was fast becoming a staple in the gambling rooms.

Professional dealers wore tuxedos. The prostitutes and anything else they requested were available to high-stakes patrons. While others had to pay for the perks, the Hotel En El Mar absorbed the cost of these guests.

Michael made arrangements to have Anthony Giuseppe live at the hotel to oversee the operations. He chose Giuseppe because he could be trusted and he would be able to handle whatever task was needed to get the job done. Guiseppe had thought it was a good time to resign his position as alderman and leave the United States for a while. Relocating was easy for him since he was not married and had no immediate family.

Fats would also be part of Michael's new foreign investment. Like Giuseppe, Fats could be trusted and was able to handle whatever task was needed. Fats had earned it. He had helped get things done, especially the transition of Jay Dies to his Miami mayoral position.

Bill Sullivan, being part of the Cuba contingency, put a number of his people from Chicago at the hotel to ensure smooth business relations with Señor Machado.

Monies would be counted each night under the watchful eye of uniformed and armed guards, provided as part of the agreed transaction between Machado, Bill Sullivan, Anthony Giuseppe, Fats, and Michael.

The months that followed became very lucrative for the Americans who controlled the casino and the high-class prostitutes, easily putting fifty to seventy thousand dollars per month into their coffers.

CHAPTER 46

By YEAR'S END, the official inquiry and investigation into the deaths of Mayor Bob Spencer and his wife, Virginia, were released:

December 8, 1925

Florida State Fire Marshal
Tom Bradley

Investigation:
House fire located in 109 block of Palmetto Drive, Miami, Florida, causing the death of Miami Mayor Robert Spencer and wife, Virginia Spencer.

FINDINGS:
Using fire patterns, it was concluded that the fire progressed from the back of the structure to the front.

Further investigation led to the fuse box located in the garage, which showed fuses blown as evidence of an electrical arc from an overloaded wall heater in the bedroom area. Here is where the wire that initiated the spark was found, causing additional wires to burn within the interior walls, back out to the fuse box.

The insulated conductors were frayed, creating overheating, melting the cloth insulation, causing wire to touch wire. This action created a huge overload of current that flowed (traveled) at great speed, initiating enough velocity and energy to burst into a flame. This flame began to burn inside the fuse box and walls. The flames rapidly spread within the garage to the vehicles parked there, igniting the soft canvas top of the Cadillac. At this point, the flames expanded to the vehicle gas tanks (where the fuel tank filler neck of the Cadillac extended outside the frame side rail), causing both vehicle tanks to explode.

Both the yellow-and-black Cadillac and dark-blue Buick were a great cause in the devastation and accidental deaths at this residential location.

State of Florida Fire Marshal,

Tom Bradley

Tom Bradley

CHAPTER 47

IT WAS A simple spring wedding at the courthouse on 161st Street, Bronx County, for Izzy and Adele Lambert, who met at Grace Bar and Grill. Adele was Izzy's favorite girl, and Izzy was her favorite customer. They both knew it from their first kiss. Adele would never kiss any of her other customers, just Izzy. It was a kiss for love, and love it was.

Michael was his best man, standing up for Izzy, and Adele had her best friend, Charlotte, as a bridesmaid.

The men wore dark navy-blue suits, and the women wore sleeveless silk chiffon dresses. Adele's dress was embellished with elaborate beadwork, which helped her stand out as the bride and added to her natural beauty. No one suspected that Adele was really not a card dealer from the private room at Grace Bar and Grill, which the story was being told about how they met. Adele would never have to return to her previous profession at Grace Bar and Grill.

Izzy had positioned himself as Michael's top confidant and good friend over the years, and as Michael would not have had it any other way; they celebrated with a small gathering of special friends along with the bride's and groom's few family members. Even Izzy's parents, who rarely left Brooklyn, decided to put their religious dogma aside to attend their only son's wedding.

The bride and groom went to the Hotel En El Mar, all expenses paid, including the wedding, to enjoy a brief stay. Izzy was to review the overall operations. Adele, of course with years of experience, would know if the hookers were all reporting their earnings, doctors' visits, and keeping everything on the up-and-up.

"This is very important for us both," Izzy said to Adele. "Michael has a lot at stake here, and we have to be sure we're not getting fucked."

"OK. I can handle it and the ladies. We'll have some fun too. Don't you want to get fucked?"

Izzy smiled. "Meet you in the room."

CHAPTER 48

MICHAEL PELL BECAME known as the gentleman bootlegger and the most successful on the East Coast of the United States, which made him very wealthy.

To keep track of his many transactions, the moneylending business was confined to New York and Florida.

M.P. Produce Expeditors was supplying most of the Eastern Seaboard and parts of the West Coast, including a contract with the US Army for apples.

Bootlegging operations consisted of barges filled with kegs leaving the Yonkers location and ferried across the Hudson River north and south to destinations for distribution, not to mention the truckloads over land.

Payrolls and payoffs were huge. Money rolled in; money rolled out. Money rolled into Michael and Regina's pockets and many others.

Much of the competition was being raided, having their entire inventory smashed and destroyed as workers and their leaders were hauled off to jail.

Much blood was shed over territories and the hijacking of beer and whiskey.

A few times someone from the gentleman bootlegger's organization had to be arrested, more for show by law enforcement, so the public could see they were doing their job. Whoever took the pinch was compensated dearly. Although there were always threats and a few attempts to kill a member of M.P.'s gang, they never came off victorious.

The organization ran by Michael was well oiled, well-known, and would retaliate tenfold, which was demonstrated by a massacre of eight men in the Thirty-Fourth Street Barbershop. Those men bore the brunt of a mistake made by rival Giovanni DiSalvo. His mistake was quite costly to himself. DiSalvo received inside information from Michael's camp that Michael would be going for his shave and hair cut at his usual barber. The bonus would be Michael's associates, Izzy and Vince would be with him as his body guards and maybe Bill Sullivan. DiSalvo, against all admonitions and attempts at persuasion from his advisors, had to see for himself Michael's demise.

Much to Giovanni DiSalvo's chagrin, his plan backfired due to the fact that Vince found out about it.

Two men imported directly from Cuba by Rafael Machado walked directly into the shop, opening fire with their military machine guns. Clothes were shredded, flesh torn, scalps blown off, and blood sprayed over the mirrors, chairs, and floor as the brown leather and white enamel chairs now cradled body parts, arm limbs on the floor, the smell of gunpowder smoke and machine gun oil chocking the air.

Giovanni DiSalvo, his four bodyguards, and three barbers—dead!

To the victor go the spoils, as in every war. Michael was well aware of the spoils he had just earned—all of DiSalvo's business. Izzy got instructions to compensate the unfortunate families of the barbers with a great deal of money, more money than each would have earned in ten years.

But he still had only one murder up to now from his gun; he still wasn't truly a gunslinger.

That one murder, however, had gotten him a reputation that had also brought with it monetary and political gains, as well as gains with law enforcement.

His reputation preceded him everywhere. The head count included those killed by his men. There were other bodies. Some were found, such as the floater in the Harlem River basin, the two in the house fire in Miami, and the eight in the Thirty-Fourth Street Barbershop. Some were not found, but all originated or followed through with Michael. He was determined never to fail, not stopping at anything that would interfere with his empire. No one really knew for sure. Maybe there were dozens of bodies.

Many others in the business had kills too. What they didn't have were the contacts and friendships that the gentleman bootlegger, Michael Pell, had.

CHAPTER 49

THE STOCK MARKET Crash of 1929 began in late October, and was preceded by a time of wealth and excess.

It was the most devastating stock market crash in the history of the United States.

This crash signaled the beginning of the Great Depression, which affected all Western industrialized countries, spreading like the lava that spewed from Mount Vesuvius, which led to the destruction of Pompeii and Herculaneum.

But as many individuals suffered from unemployment, becoming homeless, and depression so bad they committed suicide, Michael Pell continued to prosper. After all, one thing was for sure. People wanted to drink even more to drown their problems rather than face the economic turmoil and suffering all around them.

Michael knew that all things would come to an end as he recalled a great statesman, John D. Rockefeller once saying, "These are days when many are discouraged. Over the years of my life, depressions have come and gone in one form or another. Prosperity has always returned and will again."

He thought, *History repeats itself.*

CHAPTER 50

DESPERATE TIMES CALL for desperate measures.

Michael, with his entourage of Izzy, Vince, and Bill Sullivan,

visited some customers and decided to stop in at the Yonkers warehouse location.

It was a bitterly cold day in March, and the men had their topcoat collars turned up and hat brims turned down. Each gust of wind from the Hudson River cut through them like stabs from an icicle.

When their car pulled up the ramp, the guard recognized them and opened the huge doors.

Getting out of the car, they heard loud voices arguing.

Joey Adams was not there that morning, since he was taking his mother to the hospital for her breathing problems.

The two men arguing were a crew member of a barge that would ferry the kegs, and Joey's assistant, who was supposed to be able to handle situations when Joey was absent.

The four starting walking toward the loud voices. Each step closer made the arguing louder and and more clear. The barge worker was demanding more money because of the economic depression. Joey's assistant, Casper, was turning red as he bellowed obscenities.

Michael, Izzy, Vince, and Bill soon approached and stood face-to-face with the two arguing idiots. The barge idiot turned, blurting out, "What the fuck do you want?"

Casper tried to say something, without success. His head shook side to side as and he finally said, "You shouldn't have said that."

Michael, not uttering one word, turned to Vince and held out his hand. Vince, realizing what was about to happen, nodded as he reached under his topcoat, pulled out his pistol, and handed it to Michael. In one swift movement, Michael put the gun to the barge worker's head and pulled the trigger. *Bam!* The blast was so loud; they all grabbed their ears to stop the ringing. Brain particles, blood, hair, and part of an ear flew, splattering into some of the beer barrels and their clothes as they watched the worker collapse onto the floor, blood oozing down his face as if it were running from the evil that caused it. The explosive sound of the gun faded away and Michael's expression became ice-cold.

Taking the pistol back from Michael, Vince walked outside and hurled it into the cold, gray choppy water of the Hudson River, sending it to rot.

Turning to Casper, Michael said, "If anything like this ever happens again, we'll be looking down at you, sinking into the water."

Nervously, Casper squeaked out, "Ye-ye-ye-yes sir, ne-ne-ne-never! I'll cl-cl-cl-clean this mess up."

"Let's go," murmured Michael "Regina's having Charlie's seventh birthday party."

None of the deaths had fazed him, and his thoughts afterward were no longer filled with abhorrence. Clearly the paradigm of doing whatever it took to succeed had seeped into his entire being; he'd become unencumbered by any troublesome ramifications.

CHAPTER 51

OCTOBER 1929

HERBERT HOOVER, ELECTED on the eve of the Great Depression, came to the office of the presidency controlled by technicians, scientists, and technical experts. There was no political prowess entering the White House.

Once the Depression set in, Hoover lowered taxes and started public works projects to create jobs, reluctant to give outright relief. No free lunch. You had to work to eat.

Hoover's rigid adherence to conservative principles may not have been his greatest problem. A poor communicator, he came across as meanspirited and uncaring.

The single greatest policy blunder was supporting and signing into law a tariff act that fueled international trade wars and made the Depression even worse.

It's fair to say that Hoover failed to rise to the greatest challenge of his time—fixing the failing economy.

"This guy's got no street smarts," claimed Michael to his associates. "He initiates a program, and then doesn't see it to the end. He should reverse his thinking and see how the project he wants should end, then back into it, going from end to start. Then he would know what steps to take and what obstacles he may face for it to be successful. We have a fucking educated idiot for president. He's not a leader."

It seemed Michael was exactly correct.

Chapter 52

Expectations were high as Hoover began his presidency. It soon became obvious, however, that his narrow interpretation of the president's constitutional role would prevent him from taking the necessary steps to advance even his most cherished programs.

When the Great Depression hit, and millions were unemployed and needy, Hoover fell back on constitutional restraint as a reason for not allowing more forceful government intervention. Instead, he appealed to the private sector to come to the aid of the masses, while the federal government and Hoover appeared apathetic and weak.

Michael, Izzy, Vince, and Bill met to discuss strategy to deal with the downturn in the country and to make any necessary adjustments.

Michael used Hoover and his administration as the example of what not to be.

Instead he said, "We need to be like a fort that can stand up to the blows the wall has to resist. Bill, you have the contacts in Washington for the unions. See what you can do to persuade them to do whatever it takes to get more union members. More members mean more money for us. Maybe we can go to different workers, like steel, auto, and even miners. When this mess starts to turn around and people go back to work, they will need to be organized. We can help them and be paid for it!"

"Me and Mary need a few days away," Bill said. "We'll take the train to DC."

"Who do we have there?" Izzy asked.

"You remember Senator Silver from Florida?" Bill said. "He's very open to new ideas."

"Sounds good, Bill. I found out Hoover wants to meet with some of the top industrial people and the American Federation of Labor. This is where we and Senator Silver become partners. I know you can influence him toward us representing the labor union."

CHAPTER 53

As THE MONTHS unfolded, banks foreclosed on mortgaged properties. Michael bought them up for pennies on the dollar. The banks loved it and didn't care where or how the cash rolled in. They were desperate, many collapsing, losing millions.

Money was still flowing in from all the beer that flowed out, the *vig* from moneylending, and gambling and prostitution in Cuba, not to mention the revenue from M.P. Produce Expeditors totaling in the millions.

Many of the properties bought were in Manhattan, Brooklyn, and the Bronx. Michael could fill these with reasonable rents since he bought them for cash at below their original cost.

The gap between those with and those without kept growing in the country. From the first day he'd stepped foot on Ellis Island, Michael had known he would not be without.

He and his family relished in the millions of dollars that were theirs.

CHAPTER 54

PEOPLE HAD TO change their thinking in order to survive. The government needed money, and people needed jobs. Making alcohol legal again would open up jobs for the people, taxes for the government, and banks to be able to do lending.

Michael, Izzy, Bill, and Vince sat drinking espresso peppered with anisette liquor at a shop they often stopped at next to Cappelli and Sons, so Michael could say hello to Nicholas, Mama, Theresa, and Maria, although they saw one another at least once a week. Michael loved them as his own parents and sisters, greeting them with smiles, kisses, and hugs.

Bill gave the men updated information. "Senator Silver was as smooth as a baby's rump, just about telling the American Federation if they want his support and others he can bring to the table, they have to endorse Bill Sullivan to represent them. He then sort of leaned back in his huge leather chair, slowly turned his head, looking every one at the table in the eye and smiling. Each one sounded off: 'Yes, OK, I'm in,' until the entire table conceded."

"Good job, Bill," Izzy said.

"We now know why Rafael Machado wanted Jay Dies for the mayor position," Vince said. "He's importing opium into the country via the Miami ports. Dies gets all the imports from Cuba cleared without inspection."

"We did our part and are reaping the rewards," Michael said. "It's between them, whatever happens. What I don't like is Machado's knowledge of the Thirty-Fourth Street Barbershop."

"Fats and Tony the Butcher are sure that the two mechanics Machado gave us have disappeared off the island," Izzy said.

"Good, it's only Machado that's left," Michael said.

"Silver gets ten percent," Bill said. "He's got the power. We deposit it in a bank in Switzerland, where he said it can't be traced. We don't want to fuck it up. He also needs to know how difficult a person Rafael Machado is to deal with and what the situation is with his bodyguards."

"Mmmm. Why does he and the Washington politicians want to know that?" Michael asked.

CHAPTER 55

"I'M PACKING FOR Florida," Regina said to Michael. "Do you want more than two suits?"

"Yes, three. Dark blue and gray. You pick the ties," Michael answered, knowing how much Regina liked to pick his ties. It seemed to give her a sense of being connected to him.

"That's only two suits. You said three."

He walked in the bedroom where Regina was packing, coming up behind her, wrapping his arms around her waist, and whispering, "The third is my tuxedo. You will also have to pack for Cuba. Pick one of your beautiful dresses."

Regina gave a quick, shrill cry. "Yes, I love Cuba. Thank you."

"Mary, Bill, Izzy, and Adele will be coming too."

"I can't wait. I'll get Mama and my sisters to stay with Charlie." Regina released a deep sigh at the same moment Michael started kissing her neck, reaching to turn the light switch off.

CHAPTER 56

UNFORTUNATE NEWS CUT short the trip to Cuba—Regina's father, Nicholas Cappelli, had died of a heart attack at the store.

The wake, as described by Regina, "lasted for too many painstaking days, seeing Papa's lifeless body lying in a box that would soon be covered, ending a special era in our lives."

Relatives, friends, and even customers came and went, giving their respects at Costa's Funeral Home on Henry Street, Lower Manhattan. There were flowers to be taken to the grave when the time came to remove the body to the cemetery for burial.

The day of his death was a scene Mama described to everyone. In her mind, the day dragged and took forever, but in reality it was only minutes before old man Cappelli was no more. "Papa said he wasn't feeling good and couldn't wait for Sunday to have the day off and have dinner with the family. All morning he would make faces, then see me watching him and smile and turn away from me. I said he should go lay down in the back of the store. He looked at me, said OK, grabbed his chest, and fell to his knees and then to the floor. I screamed. Theresa, Maria, and Freddy came running, seeing Papa on the floor. The ambulance came and took Papa to Stuyvesant Square Hospital. The doctors said he died at the store and I couldn't have done anything."

The final resting place for Nicholas Cappelli was at Woodlawn Cemetery in the Bronx with treelined roads taking advantage of views of a picturesque natural lake. No fences or hedges were allowed, and grave markers were kept low, creating the effect of continuous rolling lawns with elegant stone monuments that helped punctuate the landscape. The canopied and ornamental trees accentuated the views and enhanced the overall romantic quality of the grounds, taking the sting of death from the minds of its visitors.

The funeral procession turned into the cemetery's entrance as Regina broke the silence.

"*Papa sempre detto che ci sono personaggi famosi sepolti in Woodlawn. Egli sarà sempre famosa per noi, Mamma?*"[1] She handed her rosary beads to her mother.

---

1 Papa always said there were famous people buried in Woodlawn. He'll always be famous to us, right, Mama?

CHAPTER 57

REGINA, AWAKENING FROM the morning light, rolled over, and realized Michael was not there. She was alone in bed with the exception of a black velvet box waiting for her. Lifting the cover, she gasped to see a beautiful emerald and gold necklace.

Immediately putting it around her neck, she walked toward the full-length mirror, admiring how magnificent it looked.

Hearing the front door close, she scurried to the window to see Michael walking toward his new red LaSalle two-door coupe. She pulled the sheer curtain to the side, knowing he would turn and throw a last glance her way to see if she was awake.

Just as she thought, he turned to look up and saw Regina standing there. He took in every inch of her naked body, devouring her with his eyes like a wild beast in the jungle devours its innocent prey.

Regina whispered, "*Tiamo tanto*," and blew him a kiss.

Michael knew Regina loved him very much. She always showed her affection for him no matter where they were.

CHAPTER 58

PROHIBITION ENDED ON December 5, 1933.

Franklin D. Roosevelt took over the presidency March 4. The Depression had been on the decline and had worsened in the months preceding Roosevelt's inauguration, March 4, 1933. Factory closings, farm foreclosures, and bank failures increased, while unemployment soared to over twelve million.

Roosevelt faced the greatest crisis in US history since the Civil War.

He undertook immediate actions to initiate his New Deal programs.

As part of this deal, Congress passed his National Industrial Recovery Bill that effectively suspended antitrust laws and compelled industries to write their own fair trade codes. The idea, in general terms, was to make each industry share the available work among as many people as possible.

Just over six months later, when Prohibition was repealed, the beer, wine, and spirits industries had to devise codes of their own.

Word about what was about to happen trickled down to Michael.

"Holy shit!" he cried with enthusiasm. "What could be better? Write our own fucking fair trade codes. We will be able to manipulate more money, power, and politicians."

Directed by his accountants and lawyers, all businesses were going to be under the direction of one company known now as Pell Global Group.

A new office was established in Midtown Manhattan, in a building owned by Michael and Regina.

Each company was its own entity but remained under the umbrella of the parent company, creating a huge legal business empire. Pell Global Group became known as PG (Pell Group), transforming from M.P. Produce Expeditors, illegal bootleggers, moneylenders, gambling, and procurers of prostitution to the following:

- Landlords of some of the most desired real estate
- Distributors of imported whiskeys, with the blessing of the government
- National produce shippers

CHAPTER 59

MICHAEL SAW THE opportunity to initiate his own new deals.

When one door closes, as it turns out, *many* other doors open.

Those employed by him who were loyal and worthy kept their positions.

"Loyalty is faith and trust to someone whose intentions are in the right place. Being loyal has its benefits, especially with me," Michael said. "I will not let happen to family and friends what happened to my mother and father, who were not compensated for their hard work, loyalty, and deaths."

Although many suffered, he did not lose a dime. Michael's life had changed traumatically since that drive to the Moon Diner in Peekskill.

His reputation was known throughout the Eastern Seaboard, parts of the West Coast, and Canada.

By growing from a produce expeditor to moneylender, to bootlegger, to controlling the Pell Global Group, Michael had earned himself an income that surpassed the seventy-five thousand dollars a year that President Roosevelt made—of course, that didn't include the millions not reported.

Michael was able to settle labor disputes with unions, with Bill Sullivan, and create political connections all the way to Washington, DC. After all, M.P. Produce Expeditors was supplying the US Army with apples at pennies above cost. Washington was quite indebted to him. They also wanted to use him to get to know the goings-on in Cuba.

Michael didn't sleep well at night. "It's from the childhood memories that plague me, not because of the economic depression," he told Regina. "After all, we are doing very well and want for nothing."

Regina encouraged Michael, saying, "We all have disappointments in our life. Disappointments build character. Disappointments make you realize that you can change what disappointed you, so you don't become disappointed again over the same thing. You get insight from being disappointed. You become a better person. If you go through life without disappointment, you are empty and have nothing. Look what disappointment has done for both of us. You're a good man. Thank disappointment every day. I love you."

Franklin D. Roosevelt's first term as president came during the darkest days of twentieth-century America, yet within three days of taking office, he had inspired the nation to look optimistically toward the future with all its disappointments.

The Pell Global Group was also looking optimistically toward the future—the company's future.

Roosevelt seized and exercised political power and became the central focus of the nation's recovery and relief.

Michael seized power financially and politically, as well as within law enforcement.

It was Roosevelt's heroic and messianic presence, not simply the New Deal programs, that was needed to revitalize the economy.

It was Michael's presence and his Moon Diner deal that keeps him being feared. Roosevelt was not without his critics, but none posed any serious threat to Roosevelt's popularity.

Michael had his critics as well as threats, but none ever came to fruition thanks to the fear of another Thirty-Fourth Street Barbershop massacre.

His popularity and reputation continued to help build his empire and ensure his safety.

CHAPTER 60

A NEW DEAL had to replace the bootlegging operation, and it did.

A group of concerned distillers met with attorneys from the Wholesale Liquor Dealers Association in Washington, DC. Their aim was to unite the entire distilled-spirits industry, write the code of conduct that would be acceptable to all, and convince everyone to sign it. The idea was that the distillers would show their willingness and ability to police themselves from within and prevent post-Prohibition bars from becoming the seedy, unregulated dives they had been prior to 1920. To a large extent, it worked.

Thus, Distilled Spirits Institute (DSI) was formed in the New York offices of none other than the Pell Global Group.

Luckily for the distillers, the DSI was going to be controlled by the Pell Global Group, which had the ability to absorb and handle the enormity of such a beast that was about to exhale fire.

Giving consideration to the warehouses in Yonkers and in Northern California, Michael knew these would be valuable in a new but similar business venture.

"I know that there is in Vancouver, Canada, an estimated 4.5 million gallons of liquor, mostly bourbon and rye whiskey, stored in warehouses awaiting official permission to ship to Seattle and San Francisco," Michael said to Izzy, Vince, and Bill. "This legalizing booze is going to work the same as we were operating, only legal. We now have the permission of the US government. We'll distribute it directly from the producers.

"We'll supply bars, restaurants, and stores. We have the warehouses, trucks, and barges. My God, we've got the world by the balls!

"Vince, arrange to dump the moneylending and gambling operations. Bill, we need to look at Cuba to pull out our resources—everything and everybody. The situation there is not looking good. You need to move fast. Get in touch with Senator Silver and give him what he wants concerning Machado that he has armed guards who can be bought. I have a feeling we're not going to have to worry about Machado and what he knows very soon."

"If it's OK with you, my brother could handle the gambling," Vince said.

"Adele's brother really could use something too," Izzy said. "I know he would be good for the moneylending."

"Both of you, set it up for them," Michael said. "We will not have anything to do with it at all. They need to understand that and not come to us when they are in trouble. They're on their own. We will be fully legit."

CHAPTER 61

SPRING 1934

MICHAEL, NOW FORTY years old, had been living the past few years in a home in the upper-class residential section of the Bronx known as Riverdale, along with Regina, Charlie, and a household staff to help with the everyday mundane chores.

The home had been purchased from silent movie star Louise Kimball, who had starred in over twenty films, acting and dancing her way to stardom on the silver screen and progressing to "talkies." This was one of two homes she'd owned, the other in California. Her early death caused the sale of this spectacular house with views of the Palisades[1] on the Hudson River. Located some 280 feet above sea level, this site was one of New York City's highest points. Regina turned it into a warm, enchanting home. Looking south, you could see a newly constructed suspension bridge spanning the river, displaying the strength, beauty, and magnificence carried by its name: George Washington.

Miss Kimball had used an Italian architect to design the remarkable Mediterranean home so it could be used for both intimate family life and formal entertaining. Regina loved doing both, using Italian interior designer Gina Ponti to have her home reach the pinnacle of stylishness. After living in so many different places, the Pells knew they were finally where they always wanted to be—in style, fashion, money, and notoriety.

"Regina," Michael called out as he was having his morning coffee.

---

1 A line of steep cliffs along the west side of the lower Hudson River creating dramatic geologic features that rise to more than six hundred feet above the river.

"Yes, Michael," Regina answered. "I'll be right there." She walked into the living room carrying her cup of coffee and a plate of biscotti, one of their favorite cookies, which her mother brought on each visit.

"I need your help. We are going to have a fund-raising event here at the house for Councilman Roberts. He is going to run for governor of New York, and he is going to have Mayor Bert Cunningham of Yonkers be his running mate as lieutenant governor. Expect about one hundred fifty guests. Ask Adele and Mary to help you. They need the exposure. Be sure to have Mama and your sisters as guests. I wish you would talk with them about turning the store over to your Uncle Freddy, selling the house, and moving in here with us. Look at this place. There's plenty of room."

"You're so kind and generous. I promise, I will."

"Be sure to get references from the caterer, and be sure the invitations say its black tie. Let Mama know that two of her favorite people promised to attend."

"Who" asked Regina?

"Her favorite actress, Vera Allen, and Yankee pitcher Jim Barry. Jim is retiring and headed to Japan for some exhibition games. The Japs love him."

"Every time Mama sees Vera Allen in *We'll Meet Again*, she cries, thinking of when she'll see Papa," Regina said, filling with emotion as her eyes teared up. She quickly added, "Me, Mary, and Adele will have a lot of fun planning this. Maybe Mama, Theresa, and Marie will help too."

CHAPTER 62

TWELVE MONTHS HAD passed since the repeal of Prohibition.

The past thirteen years had made the Pells one of the most influential families. Individuals clamored to get next to them and to be in their good graces.

Michael was in his Manhattan office waiting for Regina to arrive with Charlie to have lunch at one of their favorite spots, Empire Deli, and then go on to Radio City Music Hall to see the film *Bright Eyes*, starring Shirley Temple. Regina loved taking Charlie into the city to experience all the culture that had not been available to her or Michael when he was growing up. What she didn't like were the off-duty New York City detectives, who moonlighted as bodyguards and traveled with them for their protection. She hated it, but she knew it was a necessary evil.

One of the homicide detectives was known as John the Pipe. His reputation preceded him. Michael liked to have him around as much as possible, because he was not afraid to use what he had in order to get perpetrators to spill information. He would go into the integration room, relax, take out his pipe and tobacco pouch, and proceed to fill the pipe, lighting it. He would ask the perpetrator, "Do you know why I'm called John the Pipe?" while reaching into his inner suit jacket pocket and pulling out a slapjack.[1]

"Too many of you mistake this for a pipe…and it's not."

Wham! John would strike him across the face, then place the slapjack back in his pocket, relighting his pipe, puffing, as he continued; "Now you were saying."

---

1 Slapjacks were used as a pain compliance tool. They were black leather, flat, with lead designed to hit or knock you out. Usually they were about eight and a half inches with a strap handle and could easily go undetected in a suit jacket.

Sometimes he would tell the criminals he had to make a print of their chin along with their fingers. You could hear the other cops hysterically laughing from the outer room. Although they knew he was one of the most decorated detectives in the city, they also knew he was just plain fucking nuts.

Michael would always reassure Regina, "These are good men, doing a tough job for the people of the city."

Izzy, Vince, and Bill walked into Michael's office, knowing he didn't mind when they barged in. Usually, it was for a good reason.

"Make it fast," Michael demanded. "Regina and Charlie should be here any minute for lunch."

Izzy started. "We got word Rafael Machado was planning to overthrow Presidente Zepeda. We've been free and clear and out of all activity there—"

"We think Senator Silver took our information and put it to use," Vince added.

"Presidante Zapada found out abut Machado planning to over throw his presidency and wasn't going to ever allow that to happen.," Bill said. "They let everyone know by placing a bomb at the Hotel En El Mar."

Michael, puzzled, asked, "Izzy said we're out of there, right? Machado knew what he was in for, no matter what the consequences."

"Fats and Tony the Butcher were there too," Bill said. "They didn't want to pull out. They felt they had a future there since neither had any family. They're dead too."

Michael shook his head and grimaced, only to look up and see Regina and Charlie greeting his men, whom they hadn't seen since last Christmas.

CHAPTER 63

EMPIRE DELI WAS on Seventh Avenue, only a block away from Radio City Music Hall, which was on Sixth. Many people from different walks of life came and went. The baseball players from the New York Yankees, performers from the shows at Radio City Music Hall, the mayor of New York City with his entourage, including police bodyguards, and big-name stars that were performing on Broadway or visiting New York from Hollywood. And of course, Michael, Regina, and Charlie, along with their bodyguard detectives, who sat at a table next to them. That day, they sat down just as the mayor's police officers sat at the table next to the mayor. All the cops knew one another and talked as they watched diligently for anything out of the ordinary.

The owner, Boris Glicksman, a Jewish immigrant from Poland, circled the tables, meeting and greeting everyone in between the waiters taking the orders. As each patron ordered, the waiter sang out what was ordered and wrote it down. This was part of a show that Boris created so the customers would feel special and enjoy some entertainment. It became so popular, it was written about in the newspaper. Some of the waiters took jobs there knowing many important people would come to eat and listen to see if any waiter really had a good voice and could be discovered as the next great singer, dancer, or actor on Broadway.

Michael stared at Regina and Charlie, thinking, *I was the same age as Charlie when I came to this country. He doesn't know yet what he is going to have in life. How can I teach him what it means to struggle and earn what he wants?* Regina, taking off her linen gloves, saw Michael staring and interrupted his thoughts.

"Doesn't Charlie look so handsome in his suit and tie?"

"C'mon, Mom," Charlie said.

"*Bel'uomo giovane*; he's like his old man," Michael said proudly.

"Mom, can I have a hot dog? I love the hot dog with relish here."

"Yes," said Regina as the waiter approached, dressed in Boris's required attire: white waistcoat, white shirt, black bow tie, and black slacks.

Charlie pretended to sing along with the waiter, mimicking his mouth and hand motions. Boris approached, greeting the table.

"Always a pleasure to see the Pell family. Maybe Charlie would like a job as a singing waiter?" They all laughed.

CHAPTER 64

IT HAD TAKEN two years to get everyone and everything ready for the sweeping governor's office win.

A personal thank-you letter from the office of the governor of New York arrived, addressed to Michael, Regina, and family, from both Governor Samuel Roberts and Lieutenant Governor Bert Cunningham.

In part, it read:

> We sincerely want to thank you for your generosity and hard work helping us achieve the governor's office, as well as thanking you for your hospitality. Meeting your family was a treat, particularly Mama Cappelli. She is so proud of you both and your accomplishments, which said made clear as we chatted and nibbled on her homemade Italian cookies.
>
> Needless to say, we extend an invitation to you and your family to visit us at the executive mansion whenever possible. It is an Italianate style of architecture specifically, Tuscan influence. Be sure to contact our office staff to ensure there is no conflict in scheduling. We look forward to your visit.

Sincerely,

Samuel Roberts
Governor

Bert Cunningham
Lieutenant Governor

CHAPTER 65

THERESA AND MARIA took an apartment on Wadsworth Terrace in Washington Heights.

It was a typical area of second-settlement groups with a middle-class character. Its ethnic makeup was quite mixed, with Jews (both native and foreign born) along with Irish, Italians, and Greeks. Although quite appreciative of Regina and Michael's offer to move in with them, Theresa and Maria wanted to have their independence and be on their own since they were now part owners of Cappelli and Sons, along with their Uncle Freddy. Besides, they were moving into an apartment building that Michael and Regina owned, which in turn gave the girls free rent. This particular building was six stories, four units a floor. Theirs had two bedrooms with a step down into the living room. Regina sent over her decorator, Gina Ponti, whom she had used for the Riverdale mansion, and Gina transformed the apartment, so it looked as if it were right out of *American Home* magazine.

Mama took the advice of Regina and Michael. She sold the house, turning the store over to her girls and brother-in-law, Freddy, and moved in with Michael and Regina, very happy that Theresa and Maria were only minutes away.

Regina could not have been happier, knowing Charlie would always be in good hands with her mother around—along with the house staff, of course. Mama spent as much time as possible passing on to Charlie the family history, always speaking to him in Italian, although her Italian-accented English was quite good.

Everyone recognized Charlie would need advanced schooling being far advanced in maturity and intelligence. Mama Cappelli recognized how smart he was just being able to learn the Italian language so quickly.

"*La sua mente i fiori appaiono prima delle foglie*,"[1] she would say.

---

1   His mind blossoms before the leaves appear.

CHAPTER 66

MICHAEL AND REGINA made an appointment with Charlie to visit one of New York's most reputable private schools, which was located on the northern tip of Manhattan, only a short distance from their home. Arlington Preparatory School was a highly selective independent college preparatory school for both boys and girls for grades seven through twelve.

Usually there was a waiting list just for an interview at Arlington Preparatory School. However, with the Pells' power and status, an appointment was made available.

After a tour of the school and grounds, the Pells were introduced to Dean Harrington.

"Greetings," Dean Harrington said. "I hope you enjoyed the tour of our facility. The history of Arlington Preparatory School is one rich in tradition, scholarship, and leadership. It is a history founded on the premise that learning is not to be measured by grades alone, but by the remarkable, compassionate, and socially significant lives the students and alumni choose to lead while at Arlington and far beyond. The Arlington Preparatory School is a model, not only of traditional education, but also of sound values and truth in a changing society that is in search of both. First and foremost, Arlington Preparatory School is and has always been a school that values our children's minds, which prepare them to lead great and giving lives."

Regina, wanting Charlie to have the best education he could have, interjected;

"Both Mr. Pell and myself would be proud to have Charlie as part of your educational system, Dean Harrington. We could be quite a help to the Arlington School."

"Thank you, both," said Dean Harrington. "Our motto at Arlington Preparatory School is '*Verum values praevalere*,' which is Latin for 'Truth and values prevail.' Your support and consideration to help would be viewed as a great value and would certainly help us and the students prevail. We will arrange to have Charles take a few preparatory tests as a formality. I know you prefer Charlie; however, we address our students by their birth name. I or my staff will contact you about the start of the new school year to inform you of what to expect. Charles will have to wear a shirt, tie, slacks, and blazer. It was a pleasure meeting you both and having Charles join us on the tour. I would like to extend an invitation to you to join us as a member of our board of trustees."

"Thank you, Dean Harrington," Regina said. "I will take your offer under careful consideration."

CHAPTER 67

REGINA WAS QUITE savvy in the business world, including their real estate holdings. Being a member of the board of trustees at Arlington Preparatory School brought her face-to-face with many prominent people. There were fund-raisers, art exhibits, and afternoon lunches for the board.

Charlie was in school most of the day. He came home by four thirty each afternoon, after lacrosse practice, but since Mama and the staff were at home, Regina liked being involved in the goings-on of their wealth.

The main office of Pell Global Group was on Fifth Avenue and Fifty-Ninth Street in a six-story building that had been purchased early on by Michael and Regina. Regina had a private office there, plus personnel to help when she came into Manhattan.

She became aware of another building on Fifth Avenue and Washington Square that was for sale. The opportunity was brought to her attention by another member on the board of trustees at Arlington Preparatory School. Regina rode with Michael after dropping Charlie off at school, so she could meet with their attorney, Horace Worthington, to discuss the purchase.

"Hello, Mrs. Pell," said Worthington.

"Good to see you again, Horace," Regina said.

"Whoever turned you on to this property did you a great favor," Worthington said. "Just eighteen months ago, this would have been selling for fifteen dollars per square foot. The owners are in trouble from the market crash and can't seem to recover, so they are willing to sell for five dollars a square foot."

"Let's see." Regina picked up paper and pencil to do the math. "This building is forty thousand square feet. That brings the price to two hundred thousand dollars."

"Yes. The rent brings in forty-five dollars per square foot. That's for the rental space areas, not hallways or common areas such as bathrooms and hallways and stairs. So the total rent will bring in one million six hundred thousand dollars per year, less expenses, which will give a profit of over half a million dollars, Mrs. Pell."

"What about tenants?"

"I feel the location is great for the legal community, such as attorneys, private detectives, and court reporters since the courthouse is only four blocks away. I will take an office there myself, considering the slight discount on the rent," he said, smiling.

"Draw up the papers, and I'll present them to Michael so he can write a check. And when you submit your bill, be sure to discount it as the rent will be discounted," Regina said, smirking.

"You're very shrewd, Mrs. Pell."

CHAPTER 68

REGINA LEFT HER meeting with Horace Worthington and walked to Michael's office to say good-bye and have the off-duty detectives drive her home. She overheard Izzy and Vince talking as they were waiting for the elevator.

They were talking and laughing about someone named Casper.

"Do you remember Casper stuttering after Michael blew that guy's brains out?" Izzy asked. "'I'll cl-cl-clean this me-me-mess up.'"

Vince chuckled. "I thought he was going to shit his pants. I'm glad I threw that piece in the Hudson."

Regina, not wanting them to know she was there, kept silent, grimacing and turning her head to listen and make sense of what they were saying. *Casper, piece in the Hudson, Michael blew his brains out, clean up a mess?*

"Yeah, then Michael says, 'Let's go. Regina is having Charlie's seventh birthday party,' like nothing happened," Vince said. "Do you believe that was six years ago?"

Hearing it happened on Charlie's birthday, Regina gasped, covering her mouth quickly, so she wouldn't be heard.

"I know," Izzy said. "Casper was the last person I thought would be found floating in the Harlem River—and tied to his brother."

"His brother was a troublemaker and couldn't fight his way out of a paper bag. He used Casper to give him information he sold to Giovanni DiSalvo about when we would all be at the Thirty-Fourth Street barber shop that day. We all would have been hit."

Regina's heart was pounding, trying to make sense of the words in her mind. *Should I say anything? Ask Michael? Did he kill someone on Charlie's birthday? I know he and his business associates are not saints, but oh my God.* With her eyes closed, she clasped her hands together as if praying, raising them to the sky.

On the ride home with the detectives, trying not to think of all she'd heard listening to Izzy and Vince, Regina tried to concentrate on what Detective John (the Pipe) was saying to his partner.

"I bet you didn't know that I play the cello and love classical music. I once played with the London Symphony Orchestra. My brother, Otto, got me to sit in when one of their cello players got pneumonia. It was the thrill of a lifetime. I can't imagine how it would be to conduct an orchestra."

Trying not to give more thought to what she had heard until she confronted Michael, Regina said, "That must have been a wonderful experience, Detective. Why didn't you keep playing?"

"My old man was a cop on the street beat. He threw me out of the house and said, 'The police are hiring. Don't come back until you make the force.' I'm kinda glad he did that. Being a musician isn't steady pay. But I play whenever I can. Not too much these days, Mrs. Pell."

"Thanks for sharing that with me, Detective. I guess we all have differences with our parents never seeing eye to eye."

"Here we are, Mrs. Pell, home. Is there anything else?"

"No, thank you. Don't bother with the door. I have it. Have a good evening," said Regina, rushing into the house.

CHAPTER 69

"MICHAEL, REMEMBER, WE'VE been invited to dinner at Central City racetrack as guests of the governor," said Regina.

"I remember. Are we going for the races or for business?"

"Both. It's the Scarsdale Handicap. The governor and Mrs. Roberts will be there, along with Bert, his wife, Lilly, and Conrad Miller and his wife, Doris."

"Oh yes. Conrad Miller. He fell right into shit when he was able to purchase that racetrack up in Yonkers from the family estate. Lucky bastard."

"Bring lots of cash, so we can place lots of bets," said Regina.

"I'll bring lots of cash if you…" He approached Regina from behind.

"You'll have to explain that to me. If I what?"

Michael kissed Regina's neck, working his lips up to her ear as she closed her eyes and raised her head, to feel his breath and allow him to roam from her ear to shoulder.

"Go ahead, keep explaining," Regina whispered.

Michael, rubbing his hands up and down her thighs, lifted her negligée higher as Regina turned to kiss him, gently thrusting her tongue into his mouth, swirling it around and around his.

"Go ahead," she said, taking a deep breath, "explain more."

"I love how you use your fingers," she said as he started to rub Regina's nipples, kissing them, and then gently sucking. He moved his hand down between her legs, working the top of her clitoris, gently massaging her. She relaxed and slightly parted her thighs.

"I'm still listening. Keep explaining," Regina said with a sigh.

After helping pull the negligée over her head, Regina lay completely naked, her beautiful breasts exposed as Michael playfully tugged at her nipples with his teeth. Regina was pulling at his clothes, feeling his stiffness against her. Being fully exposed, she was grinding into the air, pumping Michael's hard cock that went beyond filling her hand as he continued rubbing her clit. Michael's erection was ready to ravish her as he slowly pressed into her, stretching her wet lips to accommodate his thick maleness as he penetrated her throbbing pussy, thrusting in and out. Regina moaned as Michael thrust faster and faster. His penis became harder, making her drip with ecstasy, keeping time with each thrust as she finished her wetness all over him.

Regina, thinking they were through, suddenly realized Michael was not, and he gently put his hands around her waist, turning her so she was on her hands and knees. He entered her still dripping wet pussy from behind, gently inserting only the tip of his shaft. He went slowly in, slowly out, not going beyond the first few inches, slowly in, slowly out then inserted all of his hard cock with strong thrusts all the way in and all the way out. Repeating it, he went in slowly, out slowly, then thrusting all the way in and all the way out. Regina, breathing heavy, yelled out, "Oh my God! *Si, cazzo! Non si fermano Sono di nuova cumming*,"[1] just as Michael exploded inside her climaxing in unison.

Michael liked to use all the tricks he'd learned from the whores at Grace Bar and Grill.

"What were we talking about?" Regina was barely able to ask before she closed her eyes and slept.

---

1 Yes, fuck! Don't stop! I'm coming again.

CHAPTER 70

LOOKING OUT AT the Hudson River through the large window of the library in their home, both Regina and Michael cuddled together, relaxing on the couch. Regina was having a glass of Chateau Clos Labarde Ducasse Bordeaux. Michael sipped on a glass of Royal Knight blended whiskey, distributed by Pell Global Group, in between puffs on his Lord Byron cigar.

Every now and then, Regina would move to accommodate his arm. The warm sun, wine, and whiskey made for a tranquil Sunday afternoon.

Regina kept thinking about the words she'd heard that day in the hallway. The conversation kept creeping into her mind over and over, so she could not concentrate on the book she was reading.

What do I ask him? What do I say? A voice inside kept saying, *Be quiet. This can be dangerous. Don't ask.* She took a deep breath, opening her eyes wide and exhaling with a deep sigh.

"That must be an interesting story," Michael said, continuing without giving Regina a chance to respond. "I want to take you and Charlie to Italy. I haven't been there since I came to this country when I was twelve." Closing his eyes, Michael said, "I want him to hear the same sounds I heard as I walked the cobblestone streets with my father. I want him to know where I came from and where your parents came from. He will appreciate what he has and, when it's time, what he will inherit."

"He's thirteen," Regina said. "He would get a lot out of seeing Italy."

Opening his eyes, Michael said, "I want Charlie to be part of Italy, not just see it."

"I love that idea," Regina said with great enthusiasm. "I'll start to make arrangements for when he's on summer break. That way we'll have plenty of time to be there. I'll have Mama write to her cousins and get information. I'll need your uncle's if you remember it."

Closing his eyes again, Michael said, "I can see every cobblestone on every street and every house on every road."

CHAPTER 71

THIS DAY AT Empire Deli was no different than any other with the exception of movie stars John Foster and Dolores Tucker, who were taking a lunch break from shooting a film they were starring in.

There was the regular clamor of cutlery and dishes, and the loud voices of the waiters singing out the lunch orders. With the addition of some extra hullaballoo when people sought out the film stars' autographs, the noise was above the usual chatter level.

Michael, Izzy, Vince, and Bill, along with the off-duty detectives who were there for Michael, always had first seating no matter how long the wait was. When the door was held open for his entourage, people mumbled as they passed. They usually quieted when the detectives casually opened their jackets so their badges and guns in their shoulder holsters were in plain sight.

It didn't matter where in the deli they sat, as long as the detectives faced the door.

Izzy asked, "How did the meeting go with the governor at the racetrack?"

"It went well. He was there with his wife, along with Bert and Lilly," answered Michael. "Conrad is a gracious host but didn't pull any fuckin' punches. As soon as dinner was through and we were having coffee, he went right to the subject of helping Sam run for president, asking for a lot of cash for his campaign. It was right at the starting bell of the fifth race."

All four men laughed.

At that moment, Michael glanced up and saw Detective John "the Pipe" furrow his eyebrows, as if surprised by what he might have heard. The detective tilted his head, apparently trying to listen.

Michael thought for a split second, *No, he can't hear us.* He pursed his lips and raised an eyebrow, deciding if what was being spoken was overheard by the detective. Michael continued speaking, but in a lower tone. "Sam would make a good president. Bert may just be along for the ride. We have a few more years. Sam has to fulfill his term as governor."

"It's never too early to start to look at this, Michael," Bill said. "Can you imagine having Sam in the White House? He—"

Izzy interrupted. "Sam will be a shoo-in for us being President. We should visit with him and create a plan."

Michael looked over at the detectives to get an idea if they were listening or just surveying the tables and the door. "I think you may be right," Michael said. "Regina is planning a trip to Italy. We'll be gone a few weeks. When I get back, we'll talk about it more."

"Michael, you look nervous," Vince said. "Is everything OK?"

"Yeah, I guess I was thinking out loud."

CHAPTER 72

REGINA WORKED HARD getting ready for their trip to Italy. She wanted to do everything herself without any help from the house staff or the office staff at PG, with the exception, of course, of Mama.

"Mama, your birthday is coming up, and we tried to hold off telling you, but you are coming to Italy with us as a birthday present. I'm sorry I have to tell you now, but we have to get your papers in order—your passport and everything else that you'll need. Our family passport[1] is only good for the three of us."

Mama let out with a yelp as she started crying. "Bless you and Michael. I haven't been back since I was a child. I was maybe a little older than Michael was when he came here. I have to pack pictures of Papa to show everybody. *Oh mio Dio! Vi benedica entrambi che sei troppo gentile.*"[2]

Regina held her mother as she tried to sob silently, knowing her mother was crying because Papa was not there to share in her joy. *"Mamma, Papà sarà con noi anche. Lui è sempre lì. Basta chiudere gli occhi e ricordare."*[3]

Mama, in between sighs, said, *"Si,* yes, yes. I know. I know. Thank you both. I'll be all right."

Regina knew how important this trip was going to be for Michael and now for Mama.

---

1 Family passports were issued to family members—father, mother, son, daughter. There was one passport holder. The passport holder may travel alone or with one or more family members. A family member who is not the passport holder cannot use the passport for travel unless accompanied by the passport holder.

2 Oh my God! Bless you both. You're too kind.

3 Mama, Papa will be with us too. He's always there. Just close your eyes and remember.

Charlie wasn't excited about the trip yet, because he was too busy finishing the school year and taking notice of the girls at Arlington Preparatory School.

CHAPTER 73

VINCE WALKED INTO Michael's office with Bill Sullivan to give him new information on Jay Dies.

"Michael, I just got a call from Jay Dies himself. There's going to be a grand jury to see if he is going to have an indictment against him for illegal activity. He asked if we can help him."

"Shit," Michael said. "That stupid, fucking, no-good—"

"Michael, calm down. I have someone who can help with the grand jury," Bill said. "He's a special prosecutor. I spoke with him already, and he said if Jay Dies testifies that it was only Rafael Machado and those in Cuba, with no one else involved, he can make things go away. He basically is telling us *Mr. Dies will have to resign and disappear, never returning to Florida.*"

Michael reached into his pocket to take out the beautiful, silver bullet-shaped cigar cutter that had been his father-in-law's. Cutting and lighting one of his Lord Byron cigars, he offered both Vince and Bill one.

"Well, that's good news," he said, smiling. "Light up and enjoy these Havanas. These were a gift from Machado himself. Can't let 'em go to waste."

The aroma from the smoke was a nice, sweet, caramel scent with a touch of buttermilk, ground black and white peppercorns, and a pinch of lime.

"Those Cubans sure know how to make a good-tasting smoke," Bill said.

"How's the plan for Italy coming along?" Vince asked.

"Regina is doing a good job with the plans and making contacts with family. She works into the night. I couldn't handle it. We leave in a week and will be gone for a month between sailing and our stay. If there is anything that can't wait, I'm sure you two can figure it out. If you think you can't, see Izzy. He has a lot of solutions up his sleeve that sometimes we don't. I've got a meeting with the Bronx Coalition to give my advice on electing a new president. They're struggling now that I'm no longer in control. On your way out, tell one of the detectives I'm ready."

CHAPTER 74

RIGHT ON TIME, both the detectives and the new Packard seven-passenger limousine pulled through the gates, into the driveway. Everyone heard Charlie cry out with excitement, "The limousine is here with the detectives."

Regina was giving last-minute instructions to the house staff as the doorbell rang.

"Charlie, let the driver know we'll be right out," Regina said.

On the ride to Pier 81 on West Forty-First Street and Twelfth Avenue, where the ship, the SS *Conte di Savoia*, would be sailing from, Charlie was talking up a storm, asking the detectives all sorts of questions.

"Do you have to shoot your gun a lot? Can I try on your handcuffs? How many bullets does your gun have? How can I become a detective? Did you ever have to shoot someone?"

"Charlie, calm down and stop bothering the detective," Michael said in a firm voice.

"It's OK, Mr. Pell. I get that a lot from youngsters. These are good questions, Charlie," said the detective, who was riding in the front seat with the driver. "Maybe I can answer all those when you come home from Italy."

Charles's asking if the detective had ever shot someone sparked Regina's memory about the conversation she'd overheard. *Those infamous words again*, she thought. *But I can't think of them now. This trip is too important.*

As everyone was getting out of the limousine, the driver and the porter handled the baggage, tagging the bags with the rooms they were going to. There was a lot of luggage from the roof and trunk, plus two bags squeezed into the passenger's seat. Mama held them tightly.

One of the detectives spoke to the ship's chief security officer, who was watching from atop the walkway as the detective approached, flashing his badge and introducing himself.

"These are very important people that I'm turning over to you for this journey. Here's a letter introducing them."

"Thank you, Detective," said the ship's officer in his Italian accent. "I see this letter is from one of your senators. I will keep this and share it with my officers to inform them of distinguished guests who will be traveling with us. We are familiar with and prepared for such guests. We've had some of your movie stars, as well as Crown Prince Umberto himself, along with his wife. On one journey, we had Queen Victoria of Spain. They are in good hands."

"Thank you," replied the detective. "I can see you have great experience. Enjoy your journey."

"*Grazie*," said the chief, giving a salute to the detective as he departed.

CHAPTER 75

THE *CONTE DI SAVOIA* was an elegant-looking ship with a sense of nobility and romance about her.

Resembling a gigantic yacht, with rakish lines that gave one a sense of speed, she represented the best of Italy's arts and culture.

Sailing day on the *Conte Di Savoia* was always a bit hectic and exciting. Anticipation was always in the air, with boarding passengers and families saying their good-byes, and celebrities and their entourages, reporters and photographers, baggage handlers, porters, company officials, and the ship's crew returning from their shore leave.

When boarding the ship, you were made to feel like you were already in Italy, before you even left the docks of New York.

The ship was christened by the Princess Marie Jose, wife of Italy's Crown Prince Umberto, before a crowd of one hundred thousand people. The ship's name was personally selected by Italy's dictator Benito Mussolini in honor of (and to impress) the ruling House of Savoy.[1]

She carried 2,200 passengers, 500 in first class, 366 second class, 412 tourist class, and 922 third class.

First class from New York to Italy was $770 per person, one way. Of course the Pells had two first-class suites, each consisting of a room with two beds, a sitting room, a bathroom, a baggage room, and a verandah. One of the suites was for Michael and Regina. The other was for Mama and Charlie. They would have the same accommodations on the return trip.

---

1   The House of Savoy is the historic dynasty of Europe, the ruling house of Italy from 1861–1946.

Everyone became more excited as they started to board.

As each person came aboard and was greeted by the staff, he or she imme-diately saw walls furnished in rich marbles, with a great domed ceiling featuring vast murals. The entry was impressive, with towering statues atop pedestals.

The SS *Conte Di Savoia* was considered the finest on the Atlantic route.

Nothing less was going to be good enough for Michael and his family..

CHAPTER 76

AFTER SETTING SAIL of their six-and-a-half-day journey, the Pells were invited to dine with Captain Enrico Pennetto, First Officer Antonio Fontana, and Assistant Chief Engineer Giovanni Caserta.

The captain's table was in the main dining area, in the center of the room. It would seat fourteen guests, but the Pells had priority seats next to the ship's officers. Other guests were seated toward the end of the table.

Although there was a captain's reception each evening, not everyone had the opportunity or privilege to dine with the ship's officers. The captain was told to surround himself with dignitaries, movie stars, and those of prominence, but he always left a few seats each evening for those sailing on the lower decks, not caring what the ship's policy was.

Everyone came in formal dress, or semiformal, out of consideration for those arriving from the lower decks.

The conversation was light as the guests shared where they came from and what they were doing in Italy or what life had dealt them.

Michael said to Captain Pennetto, "My first journey on a ship was when I came to America, and it took some fourteen days. My family—really only me, my father, and my mother—were traveling and had to stay in steerage."

"I had to sail in steerage at one time myself," said Captain Pennetto. "That's why I invite those sailing on the lower decks to dine with me. I know like you, Mr. Pell, that individuals can succeed and better themselves through sacrifice and hard work. I like to speak with them one-on-one after dinner to give them hope. So many don't have hope of change."

"It is sad, Captain, for many," Regina said. "How did you become captain of such a magnificent ship?"

"I went to the Italian Naval Academy. It was a godsend. School officials came to my hometown searching for a young boy who had the 'sailing soul' as well as tact, patience, justice, and kindness; he also had to be in need of charity. Here I am. My parents knew they would not see me for a very long time, but I chose to go to please them. Now, after many years I realize the sacrifice they made was for me."

"Excuse me, Mom," Charlie said. "Chief Caserta said he can show me the engine. Please can I go see it?"

"It's OK with us," said the captain. "We have an antirolling gyroscope that might interest him. Three huge antirolling gyroscopes were fitted low down in a forward hold. They rotate at high revolutions and were designed to eliminate rolling, a persistent problem on the rough North Atlantic crossing that affects all shipping lines."

"I remember that rolling," Michael said. "My mother, God rest her soul, spent fourteen days being sick over the rail. OK, Charlie. Stay close to Chief Caserta."

CHAPTER 77

THE NIGHT BEFORE they were going to dock, Regina got a book from the ship's library to show Charlie a map of Italy, so he could see where they would be traveling. Mama was right there to help as Michael sat on the verandah having a cigar and whiskey, remembering his childhood and listening to what they were saying to Charlie.

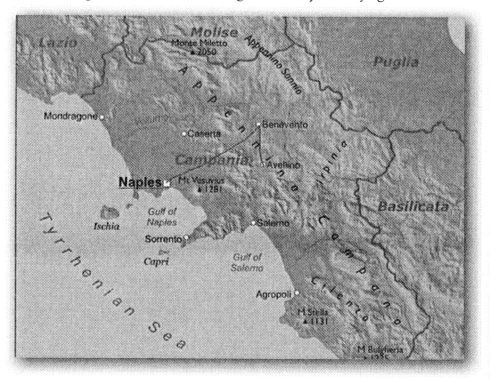

The ship docks in Naples.*

CHAPTER 78

EVERYONE WAS SO excited to finally reach the Port of Naples. As they stood on the ship's deck, ready to depart, each one looked out at the breathtaking beauty Naples offered, like the Virgin Mary who has a strong sense of life within her. She sat squeezed between Vesuvius on one side and sulfurous springs and boiling mud pools of the Phlegrean fields on the other.

The gangway looked like cattle being herded. Everyone had to move quickly to keep up with the person in front and to keep from being trampled by those behind. Many of the cattle were waving handkerchiefs to get the attention of friends and relatives who waited patiently on the dock. Suddenly, Mama Cappelli let out a loud scream of excitement.

"Oh Signore, è la mia sorella Luisa. Riconosco lei dopo forty anni. Come è bello. Luisa, Luisa, Luisa. Sono io, tua sorella, Albertina."[1]

Charlie looked up at his mother. "Albertina. Mama's name is Albertina?"

Regina was more interested in seeing the reunion of her mother and her last living sibling. Tears rolled down her face, and she had to blow her nose into a lace handkerchief.

The sisters embraced, trying to talk between sobs of joy, but nothing was really being said. The reunion seemed to last forever as the rest of the family held hands in anticipation of meeting Mama's sister, Luisa Capriglione.

Finally Regina stepped in to embrace her aunt and to introduce herself and her family.

---

1 Oh Lord, it's my sister Luisa. I recognize her after forty years. How beautiful. Luisa, Luisa, Luisa. It's me, your sister, Albertina.

A car waited to take everyone to the first destination, Benevento, a small village some fifty miles away, where Luisa lived. The visitors would stay overnight. Mama would continue her stay with Luisa when Michael, Regina, and Charlie traveled to Avellino the next day.

On the long ride, everyone listened intently as Mama and Luisa, holding hands and wiping each other's tears, could not stop talking about their lives. There was so much to impart. One would only stop, it seemed, to take a breath, then the other would talk.

CHAPTER 79

EVERYONE GOT UP when the sun rose getting ready for their next journey, Avellino.

Avellino, only twenty-two miles south of Benevento, provided a journey into nature, where the charming land welcomed you as a mother welcomed her children—with open arms.

Mama was staying behind with her sister, since this would most likely be the last time they would see each other before their common enemy, death, had its way with them.

The Pell family arrived in a car Aunt Luisa had made available, making their way right into the center of Avellino. About a dozen individuals stood waiting under the hot sun to meet the Americans, chanting, "*Cugini Americani, vi diamo il benvenuto. La nostra casa è la vostra casa.*"[1]

Michael's distant cousin, Fredrico Paglia, was the first to approach the car. Fredrico, a priest with the Diocese of Avellino, uttered words as he swept his hand, showing all in attendance making the sign of the cross.

"*Benvenutoai miei cari cugini perduti dall'America. Siamo orgogliosi di accogliere ciascuno di voi nella nostra casa. Dio benedica ognuno di voi. Ognuno di noi è un amico o un parente. Venite, lasciate che Dio vi porti a dove avete cominciato.*"[2] He handed Regina a bouquet of flowers.

---

1 American cousins. we welcome you. Our home is your home.

2 Welcome my dear lost cousins from America. We are proud to accept each of you into our home. God bless each of you. Everyone here is a friend or relative. Come; let God lead you to where you began.

Overwhelmed, each family member stepped from the car. Michael took the lead, removing his hat with a bow of his head, and speaking humbly.

"*Si, voi, mia famiglia, siete molto ospitali. Con umilta' e onore accettiamo la vostra calorosa accoglienza. Attendiamo la comodità della vostra casa e l'amore nei vostri cuori. Vorrei presentare la mia famiglia. . .*"[3]

---

3 You, my family, are most gracious. With humility and honor we accept your warm welcome. We await the comfort of your home and the love in your hearts. Let me present my family...

CHAPTER 80

OVER THE NEXT few weeks, Charlie became friends with his cousin, Benevento, who was named for the town where he was conceived. Benevento was the son of Adonis, Charlie's father's cousin, putting Charlie and Benevento somewhere on a long line of relatives. Their relationship would turn into a lifelong friendship.

Charlie called him "Benny." It didn't matter how distant they were as cousins or that an ocean separated them—cousins were cousins in the Italian tradition. Charlie's Italian lessons from Mama were paying off, and he was able to communicate easily, and he taught Benny English.

Benny could not understand why they both had the same last name, Pellegrino, but Charlie's was Pell. He thought it was just the American way, like Charlie calling him Benny.

Charlie wondered too but he didn't know why either.

Adonis had turned the family farm into a very successful vineyard after his father died, exporting his wine throughout Italy, including the two islands, Sicily and Sardinia.

Adonis was married to Mechelina Cultrera, who, with their son, Benevento, lived on the vineyard in a beautiful stone house where the Pells stayed.

Michael and Regina were very impressed with the knowledge Adonis had for business, as well as his important contacts throughout Italy. They offered to become the exclusive distributor of his wine, Terreno Rico,[1] in America.

---

1 Rich soil.

Weeks passed before Mama arrived in Avellino to meet for their journey back to Naples and the return trip to America on the same ship.

Departing was more intense than arriving. It seemed the entire town had gathered to say their farewells with many gifts, tears, and love.

CHAPTER 81

ONCE EVERYONE WAS settled in on board for the seven day sailing journey back to America, with an additional half day return due to water currents, Regina and Michael could not wait to be in each other's arms again. Because of construction going on at his cousin's house, the room they'd slept in had no door, so they hadn't been able to lie together while they were there. They were only able to ravage each other with their eyes. Regina opened the verandah doors for the breeze the same moment Michael began to tear at her clothes. It was an erotic moment of lust, not love-making. He wasted no time entering her. As fast as the ocean god Poseidon filled the room with the salty air, Michael was filling her with his manhood.

Receiving him, Regina said, "Slow down. Look at me. Kiss me softly. Do that rhythm thing you do…Oh! Yes…that's it…don't stop." She whimpered. "I love that. I love you."

CHAPTER 82

UPON RETURNING HOME to New York, Michael found that, once again, Izzy had taken care of business in the usual fashion. This time, he'd had the help of Vince and Bill Sullivan.

"No problems, only solutions," Izzy would always say.

Now he had Vince and Bill using the same mantra.

Nowadays, they had to use other means than they had in the past to keep their reputation not to fuck with their organization. Let's say they could not use Tony the Butcher as one of their solutions any longer.

Now what they used was fear.

Even though there were many more bodies that had disappeared, was that enough to instill the fear that was needed? No one was willing to find out. No one wanted to wind up like the eight in the Thirty Fourth Street barber shop.

Fear worked.

CHAPTER 83

MICHAEL HAD GOOD news awaiting him the morning he returned to his Manhattan office.

"Welcome home," said Vince.

"Good to see you back," said Izzy.

"Good news for your homecoming," Bill interjected. "I was able to get my contact I told you about, the special prosecutor, to agree to accept the papers I had forged indicating that Jay Dies's real name is Javier Diego and that he is in the United States illegally. He resigned as agreed and was deported to Cuba to avoid prison on the day your ship set sail from Italy."

"That is great news," Michael said, smiling. "I know we're out of Cuba, but don't you think we should monitor him? Are there any contacts we have that are still there? You know, why take a chance?"

"The special prosecutor said as a thank-you for what we did to help him, not to worry," Bill said. "They are deep into Cuba and its goings on with the government. He mentioned it would take at least six to eight months to finish what they want to do with him so we don't have to keep tabs on him. Oh, and the Florida special prosecutor was given to us by our friend, Senator Silver."

CHAPTER 84

THE YEAR 1939 arrived without fanfare. Mama Cappelli's health had deteriorated over the years. Theresa had moved into the Riverdale mansion to help care for her, making infrequent trips to the store. Maria stayed in the Wadsworth Avenue apartment with her husband, Frank Abruzzi, whom she'd met at the welcome-home party for everyone on their return from Italy.

Frank Abruzzi was an Italian born on Saint Patrick's Day, which many said made him the luckiest Italian son of a bitch there was. He was nondescript, indifferent, unenthusiastic, and sometimes weary. And he married Regina's sister, Maria, and took charge of the newly formed division for the Terreno Rico wine label being imported from the Adonis Vineyard, Italy.

Charlie enjoyed all the activity and goings-on in the house. He knew he would miss it when he was gone. And yet he could not stop thinking about going to Italy for the summer after graduating Arlington Preparatory School next month. He and his cousin Benny wrote to each other every week. Charlie would write in Italian, putting the English words under each of the Italian words, hoping Benny would learn faster. Benny would answer in English, saying, "Wait for you see the girls here have grown melon tits."

Charlie would laugh out loud, knowing Benny had to learn a bit more of the English language—but Charlie sure knew what he meant.

Book Two

The New Generation

CHAPTER 85

"MOM, MOM," CHARLIE called out, looking for his mother.

Regina would sometimes wonder *who that is*. That's how much deeper Charlie's voice had become.

"Benny wrote and said everyone is really looking forward to my summer stay with them. Can I ask some friends for dinner this Sunday?"

"Sure," Regina said. "Who and how many?"

"Just two, the Solofra sisters. You remember them, Maggie and Elaine."

"Yes, they were our neighbors in the old neighborhood."

"Yeah," said Charlie. "They're both graduating too."

"That's nice. I wish had known that you continued as friends all this time. You pick whatever you want, and we'll make if for you."

"I'll think about it...Ah, I know, lasagna and braciole."

CHAPTER 86

REGINA DIDN'T KNOW that Charlie would sometimes skip his lacrosse practice and go to Maggie and Elaine's house, where he and his friends grew up playing street games taught to them by their parents, relatives, and friends—stickball, kick the can, Johnny rides the pony, scully, box ball, and curb ball.

There were so many games to play and so many friends to play with, both guys and gals. Everyone thought that the fun of growing up would never end.

However, as all things do end, so did the fun street games—when the Pells moved from their modest two-level brick house on the other side of the Bronx to their Riverdale mansion.

Charlie somehow knew he was going to have to change his thinking. Down deep, he also knew he had the world by the balls. He saw his parents, their businesses, their associates, and the lifestyle they lived.

Charlie was very fond of the two Solofra twin sisters, Elaine (born Maria Elaina) and her sister Margaret (born Marguerite), known as Maggie.

Maggie won a full scholarship to the Manhattan School of Music in Morningside Heights, while Elaine was accepted to Fordham University Law School. She went on a partial scholarship, being top of her class at the Bronx School of Law and Finance, a private preparatory high school. Elaine knew she was going to be the best lawyer ever and had to work part-time to help pay her tuition, since her parents were working folks and struggled to pay for their girls' private schooling. People who fell into this type of life were known as "ham and eggers"—every day, the same old humdrum. Elaine was willing to do anything to get where she wanted to be and was not going to become a "ham and egger."

When Charlie skipped practice, he didn't go to the Solofras' house to play street games. He went for Elaine this day, as on so many days in the past. With both Solofra parents out working, Charlie and Elaine would enjoy each other's touches. Although the touches had progressed over the months, neither one ever manipulated the other without permission.

Elaine knew she would not have intercourse until she was close to getting married. But they were getting to know each other throughout many encounters, from innocent dry humping completely clothed to the encounters that became more daring.

Elaine enjoyed rubbing Charlie while he played with her vagina and sucked her breasts. As she became more excited, she would jerk his cock faster, keeping tissues ready for him to ejaculate into.

Elaine would tell Charlie, as her lips twitched slightly, betraying her inner thoughts, "Kiss me softly."

He would reply, "I'll kiss you all over, forever."

CHAPTER 87

SUNDAY DINNER THAT day was like any other Sunday dinner. That's the way Regina wanted it to be, in the Italian tradition she grew up with.

Everyone was on time for the two o'clock meal. Regina would not stand for anyone being late, and everyone knew she meant it when she said, "Sunday dinner is at two o'clock. I mean two o'clock. If you're late, don't ring the bell. Go home."

Some Sundays had more guests than other Sundays. Today seemed to be the entire family and then some: Michael, Regina, Charlie, Mama Cappelli (who was feeling up to coming to the table), Theresa; Maria and her husband, Frank; Bill Sullivan with his wife, Mary, and their son, Thomas (named after Saint Thomas, hoping that her son would be impetuous, courageous, and loyal throughout his life like Saint Thomas). Everyone wound up calling him "Sully," even his mother. The bishop was also present this Sunday for dinner, mainly for Mama. The Solofra sisters, Maggie and Elaine, were there for Charlie. Adele, Izzy, Vince, and Joey Adams were present too.

Being the same age, Sully and Charlie had become good friends when the Sullivans had moved to New York a number of years ago.

When the table was fully set and everyone was seated, Regina asked the bishop to say a blessing.

"Bless us all, O Lord, we pray, for loved ones, here and near, and far away"—Mama made the sign of the cross, eyes tearing up, *thinking of Papa and her sister, Luisa, back in Italy*—"and everyone for whom we pray. Keep us safe each night and day, the homeless who have no place to stay as well as those who are suffering in any way, the dying, those mourning or grieving, and all who need your mercy, dear God. Keep us safe, heavenly Father, when we are at home or traveling on our way, or when we are vulnerable or in danger in any way. Most merciful Father, hear us as we pray for the souls in Purgatory, or who may be sent there someday. Let the souls at this table be in your hands forever. I pray to you through your loving son, Christ Jesus. Amen."

"Amen," everyone mumbled out of respect.

"Please, *mangiare, gustare*," Regina said—eat, enjoy.

The conversation at the table was quite enjoyable. At times, there would be talking across the entire table and at times only between the people beside each other or across from each other. There was never a silent moment, due to the flow of Terreno Rico wine that Frank always brought.

Vince interrupted the flow of conversation by raising his wineglass to say, "Hey, everyone, Ray Walters called me wanting to know how many tickets we want for the heavyweight championship fight at Manhattan Arena. It's going to be a doozy with undefeated champion Billy 'Six' Armstrong versus Carmen 'The Bull' Velázquez from Argentina."

Maggie whispered to Charlie and Elaine leaned in to hear, "Who is Ray Walters, and why are those others called Six and the Bull?"

Overhearing, Jocy Adams, the ex-boxer, answered, "Ray Walters is a sportswriter, and Billy has the nickname Six because he usually knocks his opponent out in the sixth round. Carmen Velázquez looks like a bull. It's gonna be a doozy all right. Ray's the bastard—excuse me—who gave Mackenzie Mac Pharlain the nickname Smacky Mackie after I lost the fight to him."

"I don't like seeing men beating each other," Regina said. "It's barbaric, like the Romans did in the arenas."

Quickly Elaine said, "I'd love to see that. I'll go."

Silence fell upon the table. Vince looked at Michael, who shrugged his shoulders and raised his hands, palms out, as if saying, *Why not?*

"You're in, kid," Vince said. "Welcome to boxing."

Everyone applauded, followed by laughter, more wine, and conversation that became quite boisterous.

CHAPTER 88

REGINA WAS BITING her lip and saying her rosary as they drove to the airport for Charlie's twenty-nine-hour plane ride and road trip across the Atlantic to Marseilles, France, before continuing on a ten hour bus ride to reach Avellino, Italy.

In addition to Charlie's voice deepening, he had grown a few inches and was looking more like Michael, with the same beautiful hazel eyes.

"Mom, relax," Charlie said. "Tell her, Dad."

"She'll be fine. Mom always says her rosary before we fly anywhere."

"I've put some gifts in some of your bags," Regina said. "Promise me you won't forget them with the letters I wrote to everyone. You have your passport and cash. Remember to wash out your underwear—"

Michael jumped in, snarling, "Jesus Christ, Regina, enough! He'll do fine. He'll be going to college when he gets home. It's only for a month."

"Don't worry, Mom. Everything will be OK, I promise. I will send a letter to you the moment of arrival," Charlie said, looking toward his father and winking.

For this day, Regina had not wanted any off-duty detectives riding with them. She thought she might muster up enough courage to ask Michael about the conversation she had overheard concerning Michael killing someone.

CHAPTER 89

REGINA CHECKED THE mail each day, expecting a note of some sort from Charlie. She wondered why a letter hadn't arrived from Italy, thinking if he had sent anything, it should have been there already. Just then the doorbell rang.

The housekeeper was rushing to see who was at the door just as Theresa bellowed out, "I'll get it."

Theresa started to open the heavy oak door, and before it was completely open, the postman said, "Special delivery, please sign here."

Theresa scribbled her name and said, "One minute, please," and went to get a quarter to give the mailman.

"Thank you, ma'am."

"Regina, where are you? It's here. It must be a letter from Charlie. Regina?" Theresa started walking through the rooms, continuing to call out for Regina.

The head housekeeper, Rosa Mastrovanni (always addressed by everyone out of respect as Miss Rosa), informed Theresa that her sister and mother were in the back sitting library room.

Waving the special delivery envelope above her head and almost skipping into the room, Theresa said, "It's here, Regina, as in"—she burst into song—"s-p-e-c-i-a-l delivery e-n-v-e-l-o-p-e from I-t-a-l-y."

"Give me, give me," Regina said with excitement, instantly snatching it from Theresa. Looking down, she read the postage stamps:

POSTE ITALIANE, POSTA PNEUMATICA.

Each had a value of thirty lira (equaling three US dollars) two huge stamps across the front:

CONSEGNA SPECIALE/SPECIAL DELIVERY
USA

Regina ripped the envelope open, letting it drop to the floor, and pulled out the note from Charlie.

Theresa, clapping her hands together, excited, said, "Read it! Read it aloud!"

Dear Mom and Dad,

I'm so sorry this letter took so long. My travel was one and a half days that just exhausted me, and I slept for almost another day.

I'm fine and everyone sends their love and many thanks for the generous gifts. Now I've got to get to work seeing how the winery works.

Benevento is quite excited.

I probably will not write again and will see you all when I return to America.

Give everyone a kiss and give Mama two, one on each cheek.

Your loving son,
Charlie

"*Le foglie hanno trasformato in un albero forte*,"[1] Mama said.

Thinking to herself as the words formed on her lips, Regina said, "Yes, he has, Mama. Yes, he has."

---

1 The leaves have turned into a strong tree.

CHAPTER 90

MICHAEL RECEIVED A call from Conrad Miller inviting Michael and Regina to Central City Racetrack for a day at the races.

"Michael, I have something I know you will be interested in. This is business that I'm sure will get your attention. I'd love you and Regina to be here Saturday for lunch. Let's say around one o'clock. Is that good?"

"I don't see why not. I'll call Regina now to be sure she doesn't have anything we have to do or be at. Thanks, Conrad. I'll call you."

Click.

"Mr. Pell, it's Regina on line one," called out one of the office girls.

"Hey there. I was just about to call you," he said. "Is everything OK?"

"Yes, yes, Charlie's letter just arrived, special delivery. He's OK. The trip just knocked him out. You can read it when you come home. I was just so excited he sent a note, that's all."

"That's good news. We have an invite for Saturday lunch with Conrad Miller at the track. Do you have anything going on? He has a business proposal. He didn't say what but wants us to talk."

"That sounds interesting. Yes, let's go. There's nothing going on this Saturday. I have a new hat I can wear."

"Good. I'll call him back right now. You will look absolutely gorgeous in your new hat. Why don't you try it on when I get home? Just the hat, nothing else."

"Maybe," Regina answered quietly, almost feeling like someone was listening, and then hung up.

CHAPTER 91

REGINA WALKED IN with Michael, Conrad Miller, and his wife, Doris. Regina did look stunning wearing her new hat and gloves and a dress that outlined her beautiful, long, feminine frame. Both men and women turned and followed her with their eyes until she was out of view.

Once inside the clubhouse for VIPs only, the group sat at Conrad's special owners' table, with his own waiter assigned to him immediately ready to take their order.

"Four mint juleps here and see whatever our other table would like," Conrad said, pointing to the detectives traveling with Michael and Regina.

"Yes, sir, right away," the waiter said, almost trotting to the detectives' table.

"I have a great opportunity for you both," Conrad said. "It's a chance to get into racing by purchasing a thoroughbred racehorse. There's a filly I want you to look at, here at the track, in my stables. She is one hell of a filly and a beauty! I'm so excited."

They all stood to follow Conrad. When the detectives stood, Michael waved his hand up and down, like patting a child on the head, for them to stay seated.

As they passed the private stalls housing the racehorses, everyone Conrad and Doris passed bowed, saying hello.

"Here we are," Conrad announced, almost giddy. "Billy, bring her out. Isn't this filly magnificent?"

Billy Jackson, the filly's trainer, hopped to it. "Yes, sir, Mr. Miller."

"My God!" exclaimed Regina. "Look at the color of this horse. It is beautiful. I've never seen such a dark horse; she's blacker than the night. And look at the white spot on her forehead."

"Yes, ma'am, also on her bottom legs," added Jackson.

Michael was mesmerized by Regina's enthusiasm and said to Conrad, "Tell me more."

"OK, Billy, put her back. Let's go back for lunch. Leave your drinks here. We'll get fresh ones."

After getting back to the clubhouse, the waiter immediately brought lunch for the entire table, including the detectives. "I hope you don't mind," Conrad said. "I took the liberty of ordering my favorite lunch for everyone."

The lunch consisted of vegetable bouillon, veal fricassee, rice, buttered beets, and coffee with French peach pie covered with cream.

"Not at all," Regina said.

"Conrad, c'mon. You're killing me with suspense," Michael said.

"OK, here's the deal. This filly should be starting to train by its second year, which is almost here. We wait to train them because the bones don't reach maturity until the horse is four. You don't work a filly until she can handle it, starting around two. All thoroughbreds, no matter when they are born, are registered as born January first of that year and have until February of their second year to be registered with a name. It's getting close. She needs a good owner. We have the best trainer in the business and a jockey for her. What do you both think, do you want to own a race horse?"

"What are you not telling us?" Regina asked. "What does this unnamed filly cost? Where does it stay? What about the trainer and the jockey? How do they get paid?"

"Very good questions," Doris said. "Conrad tends to get excited and forget the details that are important to us ladies." She smiled and gave Regina a wink.

"It's all right, darling," Conrad snapped. "It's an investment for future earnings. This beauty is twenty-five thousand. The jockey gets a percentage of the purse. Billy gets a pittance per month and a piece of the winnings as well. Cost of stable and upkeep with fees is between three and four thousand a year. Peanuts compared to what you'll get in return. That should include vet, fees, any medicine, blacksmith, grooming, everything."

"When do you need a decision, and more importantly, what do you get out of it, Conrad?" Regina asked.

Doris burst into laughter, admitting, "Conrad never gets anything out of these deals when they come about. He loves these beasts so much, he just wants what's best for the—good, caring owners who can afford to take care of them and who won't let their investment go nowhere."

"This was most interesting," Michael said. "I'll speak with Regina in between the races and when we get home, if that's OK with you."

"Perfect," Conrad said. "That's a good start. We also need to talk about the governor for president."

CHAPTER 92

CHARLIE WOULD WAKE every morning upon hearing the roosters crowing. He would wash and get to the table to meet Cousin Benny for breakfast before heading to the winery and the fields. Benny's parents, Adonis and Mechelina, were always in the warehouse for a few hours before this, to oversee the new shipping arrangement to America.

Since Charlie was eager to learn, Benny told him about the influence of ancient empires, including the Greeks, Romans, and Byzantines who conquered the area because of such rich soil. They gave it a name: *Campania Felix*, a Latin phrase meaning "happy land."

"This, the land is big Campania," Benny, speaking in broken English. Charlie knew from his last trip to Italy and from the map his mother showed him on the ship that Benny was saying that the area was the region of Campania.

Charlie was happy when Benny introduced him to the young women working at Adonis Winery. Some of them worked in the fields that consumed acres upon acres, and some worked in the warehouse, filling the vast orders that had to be filled for distribution not only through Italy, but also now to America through the exclusive distribution of Pell Global Group.

Sophia was in charge of production, making sure the workers were wading into the fields to handpick the grapes that looked like God himself had kissed them. Beautiful, plump, and ready to harvest, the grapes had to be put into baskets, then on to carts and rushed into huge wooden vats, to those waiting to stomp the grapes in a way that looked quite hedonistic.

Sophia was thirteen years Charlie's senior. She was in charge of field production and was feisty, not taking any guff from any of the workers, men or women.

Although it was unusual for a woman to have such a prestigious job, Sophia didn't have the position because she was Mechelina's brother's wife's sister. It was because she got the workers to produce more than their quota for the day, always producing more wine than needed.

Seeing Benevento and Charlie entering the warehouse, Sophia offered to explain the process Adonis Vineyard used to produce and ship all the wine to Charlie. When she finished, she grabbed Charlie by the hand.

"Ah, Charlie. *Balla con me nei tini. Toglieteve i vostri vestiti—voglio dire le scarpe e i calzini. Arrotolati i pantaloni vieni a ballare.*"[1]

"*Stomp l'uva?*"[2] Charlie asked.

"*Sì,* yes, yes," she said, pulling him along as he hopped up and down, trying to tear off his socks with each hop.

Once in the vat, Charlie felt the squishing and heard the sound the grapes made under his feet. Grape skins got caught between his toes. He watched Sophia dancing, holding her dress up with one hand and holding his hand with the other, and he decided the movements enhanced her sexuality.

Sophia certainly knew how to motivate people. She started singing, and the others immediately joined in with her:

"*Oh Signore, che ci hai messo gioia nei nostri cuori con il vino nuovoche ci hanno mostrato cose dure e beviamo vino di scaglionare noi c'è un bicchiere in mano, Signore, che si espanda, beviamo, è il vino che allieta il nostro cuore e ci sostiene. Grazie, grazie.*"[3]

Charlie, locking eyes with Sophia, became mesmerized. She looked so provocative he became aroused. Laughing and dancing to the point of exhaustion,

---

1   Ah, Charlie. Dance with me in the vats. Remove your clothes—I mean your boots and socks. Roll up your pants, come dance.

2   Stomp the grapes?

3   Oh Lord, you have put joy in our hearts with the new wine.
You have shown us hard things and let us drink wine to stagger us.
There is a cup in your hand, Lord, it foams, you let us drink.
It is wine that cheers our hearts and sustains us. Thank you, thank you.

Charlie stopped long enough to climb out. He helped Sophia over the top of the four-foot-high vat while everyone else continued singing and stomping the grapes.

"*Ho bisogno di lavarsi. Mostra dove,*" Charlie said. Then thinking, *I should teach her English,* he repeated, "I need to wash. Show me where."

"Oh!" Sophia said with surprise. "English?"

"*Si,* yes," Charlie answered enthusiastically.

"*Venite,*" said Sophia.

"Come, *Venite,*" repeated Charlie. "Come."

"Come," Sophia mimicked.

"Very good, *molto buona.*"

Sophia guided him to the side of the water shed, where large tubs were separately filled with water, salt, dried fruits, and lemons and their juices for washing at day's end.

Charlie translated Sophia's Italian to English in his mind.

"Quickly down yours pants, loofah[4] in the juice, salt dipping, and scrub," she said. "Me, look! Turn for do back your legs you mine."

Charlie's heart was beating harder, not from the song and dance in the wine vat, but from the feel of Sophia's hand rubbing up and down his leg and up into his groin. The bulge in his undergarment had become noticeable to Sophia, who was on her knees to do a proper leg washing. She pulled his undergarment down, grabbing his throbbing cock and starting to rub it slowly. Looking up at Charlie, she started to lick his cock, which was as hard as a brick.

Charlie smiled as Sophia started to suck his shaft, putting more into her mouth a little at a time, then less, then more, like she was bobbing for apples. Once his cock was soaking wet from her saliva, she started pulling her dress overhead and dropping it on the floor, exposing her complete nakedness. Charlie never thought about the hair around her pussy being the same color as the reddish hair that fell below her shoulders but liked how it looked.

She had stunning green eyes, a light complexion, and pink breasts that filled his hand perfectly. Charlie began to touch the smooth, silky flesh, drawing her

---

4 When fully matured, the fruits become a tough mass of fiber that makes a great scrubbing sponge.

closer to suck her nipples. Slowly Sophia slid her wet pussy over Charlie's cock, engulfing him with a feeling he'd never felt before.

Sophia started grinding, pumping up and down, and using one of her hands to keep balance. She would slide side to side, then in a circular motion, all the while staring deep into his hazel eyes, which appeared like a polished gem. Charlie could see his shaft going in and out of her pussy, soaking him all down his cock and even his testicles. Charlie grabbed Sophia's arms to push her on her back, never leaving inside her. She opened her legs wide as he started pounding his body against her, making a slapping sound with each thrust, pumping harder and faster every time Sophia moaned, coming like he had never come before with Elaine.

Sophia said quietly, "*Ora potete tornare in America e mostrare la tua ragazza come cazzo!*"[5] When putting her dress back on, she used the loofah to wipe herself all over.

Charlie translated Sophia's Italian to English in his mind. "*No, no, no don't be scared. A donkey, bestia kicked me in the stomach when I was five years old. I almost died. I can never have babies.*" He felt sad she would never have any children due to a freak accident. She would have had beautiful children. Sophia told Charlie that her father paid the beast's owner 7,500 lira for the animal, and the owner was happy to rid himself of the beast, calling it the devil himself. Her father then took it to a field and beat it to death with a club, cursing it with each blow to its head.

Charlie would look forward to and savor every moment when he and Sophia bathed together and had lust-filled sex sessions. Both knew their days and nights were temporary, since Charlie's time to return to America was fast approaching, and nothing would ever turn into a lasting relationship. Charlie was happy for the bragging he could do to his friends back home, and Sophia was happy to teach sexual prowess to a handsome young man.

---

5 Now you can go back to America and show your girlfriend how to fuck!

CHAPTER 93

CHARLIE WAS SCHEDULED to leave in two days, on August 17, and wanted to squeeze all he could into the coming hours. Adonis and Mechelina were holding a farewell dinner in his honor at the main house. Those invited were friends, some workers, and their long-distance cousin, Father Fredrico Paglia, along with, of course, Sophia.

Michael and Regina were glad Charlie was leaving Italy. The news they wee receiving about what was going in Italy with Fascism was very concerning.

Charlie's dinner celebration started with Father Fredrico Paglia offering a blessing, which he concluded by pointing out that "God allows the grass for cattle; he also allows bread to sustain man, and of course wine that cheers man's heart."

In unison, everyone said, "Amen."

Benny seemed a bit nervous during the meal and was anxious for it to be over. Charlie himself felt the same way, since he wanted to leave and eventually sneak to be with Sophia, but he had to remain respectful. As the evening drew to an end, everyone was on their way out. Sophia signaled to Charlie with a tilt of her head, motioning two times to meet her. She puckered her lips, indicating a quick kiss.

Benny pulled Charlie to the side and whispered, forgetting his English, "*Dillo a Sofia, nel mentre si deve aiutarmi a spostare qualcosa.*"[1]

Charlie did just that, saying his thank-yous and good-nights, letting Sophia know he would be late. Adonis and Mechelina were going to spend the next day doing last-minute visiting with Charlie and Benevento.

---

1 Tell Sophia that you have to help me move something.

Benny took Charlie by the arm and led him away from the house, telling him why he needed him.

"I your help, need a body bury," Benny said.

"What the fuck do you mean? A dead body?"

"*Si*," Benny said, "not dead yet. Going be soon with your help!"

Complete silence engulfed them both.

After walking a few minutes, Benny started to tell Charlie why he needed his help to do this deed.

"I never did this before," Benny said. "We hired a man who is a drunken pig Fascist. We did not know it then. He worked in the vineyard and stole the formula how to make the wine. I caught him."

Charlie, surprised, asked, "Why don't you call the police?"

Benny had a fast burst of laughter. "The *polizia*? No, no! Them one month, maybe to bother. I have him tied in watershed. You will distract him."

"Distract him, how?"

"He is tied to post standing. I really tied him. You talk to him, ask questions as if you are *polizia*." Just before opening the door to the shed, Benny gestured to Charlie and said, "Give me your belt."

Charlie obliged, undoing the belt buckle and pulling the belt through the loops, handing it to Benny.

Benny picked up the lantern, lighting it as Charlie opened the door. The darkness was immediately dispelled by the lantern's glow. There stood an older man tied to the pole, a rag stuffed in his mouth that was held in by a donkey's bridle

Charlie began questioning the man, who had become the town drunk that no one cared about, always chasing him away because he begged or tried to steal, not wanting to work. No one knew if he had a family or really cared if he did have a family.

Charle continued to question the man in Italian. He still seemed to be drunk. "What were you going to do with the information you stole?" He loosened the man's gag.

Slurring his words, the man took a deep breath and sighed. "Don't arrest me. I needed money. I would sell." Charlie translated as fast as he could, trying to make sense of it all.

At that point, Benny went behind the pole, wrapping Charlie's belt around the man's throat, pulling it as tight as he could, putting his foot against the pole to give him leverage. "*Guida, rapida,*" he commanded Charlie.

Charlie went around to grab the other side of the belt, and they pulled together. The drunk making a gurgling sound as his eyes started to bulge; then there was no more life in him. He went limp.

Charlie snorted, mixing Italian and English. "Holy shit! Benny. *Ora che cosa...now what?*"

"The cart is ready. I have it hooked up to the mule. Take shovel and throw it in the cart and come back. Quiet," Benny said, holding his finger up to his lips. "Shh!"

"What the fuck is that smell?" Charlie bellowed.

"*Shh! Egli merda i pantaloni!*" exclaimed Benny in a whisper.

Charlie did as Benny instructed, coming back so they could put the dead man in the cart and asking, "Where's my belt?"

CHAPTER 94

CHARLIE AND SOPHIA barely slept, using every moment to make love through the night over and over—sometimes with aggression and other times with tenderness. Charlie didn't want to say good-bye to Sophia.

"I am really going to miss you. Not just, you know. I'll miss you."

Grabbing Charlie's face, her hands on each side of his cheeks, looking into those gem like hazel eyes, she said, "Charlie, *mi mancherai come non ho mai perso un uomo nella mia vita. Abbiamo vite diverse nei l'oceani. Saremo entrambi amare un altro in un modo diverso. Go. Sarai sempre speciale. Non scordar mai di me! Ti amo.*"[1]

---

1 Charlie, I will miss you like I've never missed any man in my life. We have different lives across different oceans. We will both love another in a different way. Go. You will always be special. Don't ever forget me! I love you.

CHAPTER 95

CHARLIE'S RETURN FROM Italy was without any fanfare. He knew he had to spend time with Mama as she continued to wane; she now had a full-time nurse with her. He also knew he wanted to spend time with Elaine and Maggie. The last weeks of summer weighed heavily on each of them, since they didn't expect to be together again as a threesome for a long time. Each of them was planning a future in a different direction. Charlie, still not knowing exactly where he was headed except to Boston for school, was a little jealous that the Solofra sisters had it together. One thing they all knew was that September would roll around fast, so they wanted to squeeze whatever they could into the time left. Each day was a trip to Orchid or Jones Beach and Fire Island. Charlie would drive to Fordham and pick the sisters up.

Their nights were either City Island, Manhattan, or a ride up to Island Casino, a unique jewel situated way up the line in Westchester County. It was originally created in 1879 as a summer resort for a businessman named John H. Starin. The place was a springboard for big bands and singers. The casino happened to be one of Charlie's father's customers during the bootlegging days, when they also had illegal gambling. Pell Global Group continued to service Island Casino with wine and liquor, legally now.

Charlie knew 52nd Street very well. Nightclub after nightclub lined the street. With Prohibition long over, Charlie knew these clubs still had plenty of nightlife. These too had been his father's customers during that era of no booze. Charlie would take his father's new Packard with its front air suspension. When the car was parked, Charlie would have Elaine and Maggie sit on the front fender.

"C'mon. Sit on the fender," Charlie urged. "See what happens."

The car would dip down, then all of a sudden would rise up with a hissing sound to its original position. The girls would hop off, laughing.

"Charlie, you are fun to be with," Maggie said as she slid off the fender and landed on her ass, laughing.

CHAPTER 96

THE NIGHT DREW to a close, and it was time to drive home from Manhattan. You could see the stars glitter, putting on a show for anyone who looked. The piers were filled with people trying to keep cool in the river's breeze. Many of them came from the surrounding apartment houses, which were hot and stuffy. There were people sitting on their fire escapes or just hanging out the windows leaning on pillows. Charlie recalled how his father would tell of how he and his mother loved to go to the pier on South Street to enjoy the East River's summer wind.

Charlie pulled over and parked. Maggie was asleep in the backseat. Elaine and Charlie got out and walked the pier. They could hear the chatter of the people in both English and their native tongues. Charlie noticed how Elaine's toilet water perfume was intoxicating. It matched the soft, summer, spaghetti-strap dress against her beautiful olive skin. She was magnificent. They stopped, turned toward each other, and shared a kiss that sent tingling up Elaine's spine.

"Oh God, Charlie. What does this mean?" Elaine asked nervously. "We've got too many roads ahead of us." The words tumbled from her mouth. "I know what we do sometimes, but—"

"Boy is it hot," Maggie called out, walking down the pier barefoot toward them. "What are you two doing without me, trying to fall in love? C'mon, let's get going. Fall in love later."

CHAPTER 97

SEPTEMBER ARRIVED WITH a beautiful Indian summer day.

Charlie always saw the months of the year and the days of the week in his mind as colors. September was gold month. It was Sunday, the color yellow. A gold month on a yellow day. This meant good things to Charlie, two bright colors bringing a new month. It was sort of like what his father did with numbers. He picked up the phone to dial Elaine.

"Hello."

"Elaine, its Charlie."

"It's Maggie. Elaine ran to the store to pick up bread for dinner. C'mon over and join us. Mom and Dad went to the island to see Grandma."

"I'm sorry. I heard she's not doing well."

"Listen," Maggie said as if Charlie hadn't said a word. "I'll tell Elaine you'll be here around six to join us for dinner."

Click.

Charlie dismissed the abruptness that was usually associated with Maggie.

CHAPTER 98

AT DINNER, THE three sat talking about their hopes, dreams, and ambitions. Charlie knew that Elaine was going to Fordham Law and Maggie to the Manhattan School of Music to study violin, wanting someday to be first violinist for a symphony orchestra. Charlie announced that he was going to a Boston school for business. He saw the disappointment in Elaine's eyes until he reassured them both that he would be home often. Elaine got up to start to clear the table. A moment later, Charlie followed.

As he went through the swinging door, he grabbed Elaine, turned her, and started kissing her neck. She grabbed him by the side of his head, passionately kissing him and thrusting her tongue down his throat. They both heard the front door slam but didn't pay much attention to it as Charlie's hand quietly went into Elaine's dress and started to undo her bra to caress her breast.

"You smell so good, Elaine."

"It's Lux soap."

Elaine's skin was soft and warm as Charlie gently felt her nipples rising. Their heated tongues met, both working on each other's lips, probing gently as if inviting each other, begging for sex. Their knees buckled as they fell to the floor.

It seemed that their clothes melted off in an instant. Both were completely naked, wrapping their bodies around each other.

Charlie opened his eyes to see something that was more breathtaking than anything he had imagined. It was even better than when they had been together before he had gone to Italy and much better than the pictures he'd used to masturbate in the girly magazines he had bought and hid in his bedroom. And more beautiful, yes, than Sophia.

Charlie remembered everything Sophia had taught him. Elaine was more nervous than Charlie as she pulled him toward her. He started to caress her breast. This time Elaine said, "Your hands feel good and warm."

Elaine started rubbing his erection. Charlie felt her nipples rise and his cock get harder as he proceeded to tease her pussy as Sophia had taught him. Elaine thought, *this is much better than what we used to do.*

Charlie became thick and hard. He knew he wanted to be gentle and continued to finger her clitoris as her pussy got wetter, opening it wide with his fingers. Elaine started to give a moan as she felt a warm sensation wanting more.

Elaine could not take it any longer. Almost begging, she moaned, "Fuck me."

As Charlie entered her, he knew she was amazed by her body's reaction. He felt her toes curl on his legs as she pulsated with each thrust of his hard cock, his finger still rubbing her clit.

"Don't stop. Yes, go, go." Elaine arched her back to confront each thrust, grasping Charlie's back.

Her eyes rolled back in her head. She had not a care in the world as she embraced every second of her explosive orgasm. They both weakened with each pulse that spurted their hot fluids.

Elaine, in between breaths, softly said, "I want you in my life."

It was the first time for Elaine.

CHAPTER 99

THE WEEKS FLEW. Charlie and Elaine kept their dreams alive, always making the time for each other. Even though summer was supposed to be time away from school, both Maggie and Elaine always took extra credits. Their parents were uneducated, like so many of the older generation, and both families were determined to have their children go on to college, which would be greater than what anyone they knew could and would accomplish.

Charlie had settled in at the dorm in Boston. He had his class schedule for fall, which was officially starting at the end of October.

Having some time to himself until classes started, he headed home to be with family and Elaine.

CHAPTER 100

THE UNITED STATES was the undisputed center of the boxing world, even during the lingering economic peril. What was cementing the American hold on the sport was financing. Foreign countries did not have the money backers, so fights and fighters followed the money, and most of the money was in the United States, so Carmen Velázquez was fighting in the United States, even though he was from Argentina.

The huge poster in the lobby of the Manhattan Arena hit you right in the face.

THE MANHATTAN ARENA PRESENTS

THE BIGGEST FIGHT OF THE DECADE
Friday Evening, October 7

Billy "Six" Armstrong
Vs.
Carmen Velázquez, the Argentina Bull
WILL IT GO THE DISTANCE—15 ROUNDS?
OR WILL BILLY DO IT IN 6? NO GAMBLING ALLOWED

CHAPTER 101

MICHAEL ENTERED THE arena with his entourage.

It was mostly filled with men puffing on cigars. Some were there with their wives, some with the hookers from the Grace Bar and Grill.

Elaine was enthralled by what she saw, and she pulled Charlie close to her, almost having to shout over the chaos. "I love this. I want to come to one of these again!"

Charlie smiled as he squeezed her hand. "Me too. We can always get good seats."

Elaine wanted to know every detail she was witnessing. "Why are so many people waving money in the air?"

Charlie couldn't hear what Elaine was saying, but Adele, on her other side, answered, "They are going to bet on which fighter they think will win. The men taking their money are writing down who they are and who they are betting on and for how much, so when the fight is over, they either lose their money or win, depending on what the odds are for the fighter they bet on. Understand?"

"Wow! I do. It's exciting," Elaine said with wide eyes, taking it all in.

Adele grabbed Izzy's arm and pulled him toward her so he could hear.

"This Elaine seems to fit right in with the family. She's a winner."

They all made their way to the second and third rows, which was better viewing than the first row because they could see without tilting their heads and getting cricks in their necks.

The crowd roared as the two challengers walked down separate aisles in their silk robes, followed by their trainers and handlers marching as if they were in a parade. They entered the ring and went to their respective corners.

All of a sudden, a microphone dropped from the ceiling, its long wire right on target into the announcer's hand just as a bell rang to get the crowd's attention. There he stood with notes in hand, dressed handsomely in a black tuxedo.

"Ladies and gentlemen," the announcer said. "Welcome to the main event. Fifteen rounds for the Heavyweight Championship of the World. Presenting in this corner"—he pointed to his right—"the challenger from Argentina, weighing 234 pounds and wearing blue-and-white trunks, the Argentina Bull, Carmen Velázquez. In this corner"—he pointed to his left—"weighing 229 pounds and wearing red trunks...the reigning champion, Billy 'Six' Armstrong."

The crowd cheered and rose out of their seats when their champion was announced. The referee brought the fighters to the center of the ring with their handlers and trainers to review the rules of the fight, then all retreated to their neutral corners.

The bell rang to start round one. Reporters were taking pictures, with flashbulbs blinding the eyes of the crowd. The boxers started toward each other.

The announcer began. "The fighters are dancing around each other like a choreographed ballet with a quick right hook from Velázquez, back to dancing, grabbing and holding on to each other to help wear the opponent out. The referee separates them. Jab, jab, left hook to the face from Billy 'Six' Armstrong as Velázquez grabs and holds Armstrong around the back of his neck, continuing to punch him with repeated left uppercuts to Armstrong's jaw."

The bell rang.

The announcer said, "Round one is over."

Elaine turned to Charlie. "What's happening? This is so exciting!"

Charlie explained. "Each round is only three minutes. They go fifteen unless one of them drops or the ref stops the fight."

Ding, ding. The bell went off for round two. Both fighters charged each other until they were toe-to-toe.

"Armstrong throws a smashing blow to Velázquez and another to his ribs," the announcer said. "Velázquez stumbles backward, losing his balance and falling to the canvas. The referee pushes Armstrong, pointing him to his corner so he can start the count on Velázquez, who is on the canvas."

The flashbulbs from the reporter's cameras became as bright as a full moon on a clear night.

"Why is he counting?" Elaine asked.

"If the fighter stays on the canvas and can't get up by the count of ten, he loses the fight."

"The Argentina Bull is down, folks," the announcer said. "It looks like he is getting up on the count of four. The referee is shaking his gloves to see if he is OK. All right, they're back at it. A little blood from his nose. Look at Armstrong charging him. He should be the bull. Wow! Did you see that right hook to Velázquez? He's stumbling again. There's the bell. Round two just ended."

Elaine grabbed Charlie to turn his face toward hers and gave him a kiss, whispering, "This is exciting and—"

The bell rang.

"Round three begins, ladies and gentlemen," the announcer said. "They're throwing punches wildly. I don't know how the judges can keep up with who is striking who. Velázquez only has a five-pound difference over Billy, and it doesn't seem to be in his favor. What's in Armstrong's favor is the three-inch reach he has over the Bull. A left hook by Billy Six just shook up Velázquez, who is now on the ropes trying to hang on to Armstrong. The referee is breaking them apart."

Ding, ding. "Another round ends, ladies and gentlemen."

Ding, ding. "Round four here at the Manhattan Arena. A quick right from the Bull to Billy's ribs. He sure is powerful, and you know you're hit when the Bull's fist hits you. I look around and see a few important people in the audience. Billy Six won the championship two years ago, and he trains hard and long. Not like Joey Adams, who never trained and lost to Mackenzie Mac Pharlain, better known as Smacky Mackie. He's here tonight, folks. That is, Joey Adams. I see him here with a lot of important people including...Wow! Did you see that? Two left hooks to Velázquez. There's Ray Walters, the sportswriter who gave Mac Pharlain the name Smacky Mackie. Joey didn't like it at all. They're here together tonight, so I guess they're friends now. Armstrong is the favorite as the incumbent."

Ding, ding. "The stools are down in their corners as the trainers' check their eyes and the fighters are being sponged down. Velázquez pushes the handler's hand away, trying to stare at the opposing corner while his trainer sticks gauze up his nose to stop the bleeding before the bell rings and he has to remove it."

Ding, ding. "Round five. What's going to happen? Will Billy Six have to go the distance? It doesn't look like Velázquez is tiring. Oh! A right cross and a left hook to Velázquez. Did you see that? He's down and up on the count of two. The ref is checking him. He's OK. Armstrong has never even been knocked down in his career. The crowd is cheering 'six, six, six, six,' hoping Billy can do it. Velázquez is getting a few blows to Armstrong, but it doesn't seem to faze him. My guess is Armstrong's manager told him during the bell to go in strong. Look at Billy! He is going in strong. My God! Two left hooks, no three. The crowd is on their feet. The Bull is down. Armstrong goes to a neutral corner. The crowd is absolutely wild. Six, seven, eight, nine, ten! *He's out!*" shouts the referee, waving his arms. "Billy Armstrong did it again by the sixth round, ladies and gentleman. The time was seventeen minutes and forty-two seconds. The winner and still world heavyweight champion, Billy Six Armstrong. The referee is holding Billy's hand high in the air, showing he won. You can't even see Velázquez. The doctor is bending over him. There he is, folks; he is standing and quite shaken up as he makes his way to congratulate Billy. Now that's a true sportsman. Billy announced in last week's newspaper that he is thinking about retiring after this fight. Velázquez and his team sure want a rematch, but only Billy can make that decision. Thank you and good night."

The crowd was just going wild. The police were all around the ring as people pushed, trying to get in with the fighters while they were trying to get out of the ring.

The Pells' bodyguards surrounded them as they pushed their way to the exit. Elaine kept looking back at Charlie, who held his hand on the middle of her back, guiding her along.

"Charlie, I'm hot for you," Elaine said. "We need to go find a place when we get back." Charlie kept lowering his hand, rubbing her lower and lower as they continued making their way out.

CHAPTER 102

MICHAEL AND REGINA were excited about owning a thoroughbred racehorse. Regina was in charge of picking the silk colors the jockey would wear and picking the name that had to be registered. All the legal details were left to Horace Worthington.

Charlie was back at Boston for the new school semester. The racehorse was going to be a surprise. They didn't want to tell Charlie until all the details were finalized.

To include her mother and sister, Regina asked, "Mama, Theresa, what colors and name do you like for the new racehorse?"

"From my astrology and tarot cards, I found yellow; bright yellow, a positive color closest to pure light; and green, which symbolizes life, growth, and rebirth," Theresa said. "I like them together. If you can add a symbol, put circles."

"Why?"

"Circles represent unity. They are without beginning or end, sides or corners, and can be associated with protection and the number one."

"Yes, that's it," Regina said. "We want to be the number one horse and win. That's what we'll use, bright yellow silk with green circles. Now all we need is a name."

Mama was enjoying the view of the Hudson River while sitting in the library with Regina and Theresa. They were waiting for the nurse to return from the kitchen with tea and medication for Mama.

"Why not call the horse Nick's Arrow, after Papa?" Mama said. Regina and Theresa looked at each other, shrugging their shoulders, both thinking, *why that name?*

Mama went on without noticing their reaction. "Your father would always keep moving forward so we would have a better life for all of us. Like an arrow."

"That's perfect, Mama."

"Here is your tea and medication," interrupted the nurse.

"We will use the colors and the name. I have to call Horace to let him know. Thank you, both."

CHAPTER 103

CHARLIE, ELAINE, MAGGIE, and Sully settled into their own routine with their school schedules. Elaine and Maggie, being local, would be home each night. Maggie had more time than Elaine, since her full scholarship meant not having to work. Elaine had to work part-time some evenings and Saturdays as a clerk at the women's perfume counter in Franklin's, a very busy department store on Fordham Road close to the university. During the summer, she would intern at the district attorney's office on 161st Street.

Charlie and Elaine mailed notes to each other at least once a week. They always included how they couldn't wait to be together.

One of Charlie's notes read, "I want to touch and kiss and lick you from head to toe, all over your luscious body. I want you to hold me like you won't let go as I lick and kiss and lick. Then I want you to put me inside you, slowly, until I fill you. I want to feel your soft lips on mine. I really miss you, Charlie."

Elaine responded in a similar manner: "Charlie, I can't wait either. I'm so happy we have such feelings for each other. I want you to enter me and fill me with your manhood. I did not know it was possible to get better every time we love each other the way we do. Remember the last time when we got home from fight night at the Manhattan Arena? I was as hot for you then as I am now. Tell me when you get a break and will be home. I miss you too, Elaine."

Each of Elaine's letters would be sprayed with perfume from the counter where she worked before mailing it off.

Charlie wrote to Benny and Sophia in Italy at least on a monthly basis, keeping in the back of his mind that he wanted to take another trip someday. Charlie would write to both in Italian, and they would answer in English as best they could.

Sophia would write with not much to say but with much improvement with her English.

"Dear Charlie, We busy at work. Adonis Wine growing. Your company keeps all busy. Me happy make extra lira. I think of you, Sophia."

CHAPTER 104

REGINA ASKED THERESA to direct the staff to get the house ready for the visit of Governor Roberts; his wife, Priscilla; and their two state trooper bodyguards, along with Senator Silver, who would have a brief stay.

"You and I will have to keep Mrs. Roberts entertained," Regina said.

"Ought to be kind of fun being friendly with the governor's wife," Theresa said.

"Who knows?" answered Regina. "More fun if she becomes the first lady."

"I'll be on my best behavior," Theresa said, smirking and chuckling a little.

CHAPTER 105

DECEMBER 21, FOUR days before Christmas, was the only time everyone could schedule the meeting with Governor Samuel Roberts, Michael, Bill Sullivan, Conrad Miller, and Senator Silver from Florida. It was to be held at the Pells' Riverdale mansion. The timing allowed everyone to be home a few days before the holiday.

Regina had their home decorated for Christmas with the help of Gina Ponti, who had become a friend as well as her decorator. Entering their home was like walking into a mystical wonderland. The first sight was a huge evergreen tree decorated as if it could be used in a magazine ad, with wrapped presents all around it. Garland carefully wrapped the staircase spindles. The air outside was crisp, as if it were electrified. Snow had fallen some days before. Riverboats passed, their lights glowing both day and night, adding to the spirit of the holiday season. Gina was able to purchase a special wood for the fireplace that gave off the aroma of a pine forest, adding to the magical feeling.

After a buffet lunch, the gentlemen moved to the sitting room overlooking the river while the women visited in the living room. The state troopers who always traveled with the Govorner played cards in the kitchen. "Very simple, Sam," Conrad said. "We're here today to let you know we feel you'd be a great candidate for the presidency."

Senator Silver chimed in. "I will get all my friends in the Senate to influence other friends both in our party and outside to back you. I'm here in person to look you in the eye, Sam, to say you have a very good chance of pulling this thing off."

"We can raise a shitload of money for your campaign, Sam," Michael said. "Look, you know, as we all know here, what could be done for all of us and many others throughout the United States if you become president. We also know all the money that will be brought back to us all from the influence you will have to get new laws passed. We're talking millions of dollars, Sam."

"I have the unions, and they will back you as well. You've seen our power in the past with these issues," Bill said. "What are your thoughts, Sam?"

"I'm being frank with all of you," Sam said. "We all know our past and what all of you have been involved with. I've been there with all of you. How can we squash or keep all of that shit from coming up? We will have a lot of people to answer to who will want something in return for their part in helping this come full circle. Can you, we—you, Conrad, or you, Senator—handle the heat if it comes up? Can any of us?"

"Michael?" Conrad asked.

"Everyone who can or will drag up past history will think twice about it. If anything, it will be some hotshot reporter trying to make a name for himself, and when he does, Conrad has contacts with the newspapers. Conrad will do a preliminary meeting with his contacts, yes, Conrad?" Michael replied.

"I believe it should be a simple task, and I can start on it as soon as we get a commitment from you, Sam," said Conrad.

"Nothing happened when we were behind you for the governorship," Bill said. "If anyone had been able to come up with any dirt, they would have done it then. Keep that in mind, Sam."

"I believe it shouldn't be a problem," the senator said. "We know there are going to be a lot of favors to certain people. If they want their favors, they're not stupid; they'll make sure no bullshit will be brought up. There's a lot of power here in this room, Sam. Don't discount it. We all will benefit."

"I believe this was a good meeting, being able to look at each other face-to-face," Sam said. "It helped settle some thoughts I was having. I'm going to have to speak with Priscilla so she can prepare for the turmoil and hard campaigning that will be expected. Who will be my running mate?"

"This is only a preliminary, Sam," Michael said. "We have a lot of time, months and months. It maybe a couple of years. We'll have to have a lot more meetings with a lot more people as to who will do what and in what capacity. This is a slow-working machine with many cogs in it. Let's join the ladies in the living room."

"I've got to catch my flight back to Florida, but first I'll have a whiskey with everyone," Senator Silver said.

Michael headed to the kitchen to let the state troopers know to drive the senator to the airport and to that Govoner would be ready momentarily as well. Michael walked the troopers to the door, handing them each an envelope filled with cash.

"Merry Christmas, boys," Michael said.

CHAPTER 106

MAMA'S HEALTH WORSENED. The doctors strongly suggested that she be moved to Mother Cabrini Nursing Home, where she would get the attention she needed at a full-service facility with full-time doctors, nurses, and nuns.

As sad as it became, the family knew it was necessary and made the arrangements for her transfer as well as getting all her affairs in order. They called in Horace Worthington to handle all the legalities to be sure all the t's were crossed and all the i's were dotted.

Michael assured Regina, telling her, "Be sure whatever there is in your mother's estate goes to your two sisters only. I think Maria and Theresa should sell your uncle Freddy their share and give him full ownership of the store, and have Theresa become your assistant. Maria can be put on the payroll in the winery distributorship with Frank. What do you think?"

"I'll meet with them both after we get Mama settled at the nursing home. I think it's a wonderful idea. I don't see why they wouldn't like that idea. I love you."

"Let Theresa know she can keep living here. I'm sure she doesn't want to move back in with Maria and Frank."

CHAPTER 107

CHARLIE CAME HOME from Boston in early spring to see Nick's Arrow perform her first professional race at Central City Racetrack in Yonkers. Elaine and Maggie joined Charlie, along with Sully. Conrad Miller's clubhouse VIP room was crowded, not only with the Pell family and the people who traveled with them, but also with the press, photographers, runners to take the bets to the betting windows downstairs, waiters, and sports announcers.

The clamor, noise, hustle and bustle, the lights of the betting odds board changing were only parts of the excitement.

"Hey, c'mon. Let's go see Nick's Arrow and meet the jockey who's riding this magnificent animal," Conrad said. "Follow me while our room and table are being set."

Approaching the stables, they could hear the horses neighing, and see the jockeys shining their boots and the trainers brushing and primping animals, checking the saddles and bridles.

"Hold her down while our company gets to know her," Conrad said to her trainer. "Billy, you remember the Pells?" Billy tipped his hat as a greeting.

"Eddie, where are you?" called Conrad. "Ah! There you are, Eddie. Meet Mr. and Mrs. Pell, their son, Charlie, family and friends. This is Eddie Hudson, one of the best, if not *the* best jockey in the racing game. Eddie, tell everyone how Nick's Arrow has been doing."

"It's a pleasure to meet you all," said Eddie, shaking everyone's hand, including the ladies.

Eddie was just as a jockey should be: about four foot ten, weighing in with his full uniform, boots, and whip at 115 pounds.

"I love how the colors and design turned out," said Theresa. "She looks kind of cute."

"Well," Eddie said, hearing Theresa's comment and smiling, "she sure can be a winner. She's been runnin' real good times and is holding up real good. This is the filly's first run at a real race. When we ran her with others from the stable, I was impressed. I will ride her to be a winner. I can assure you that. I want to be in the winner's circle too, you know."

"Good luck, Eddie," could be heard over and over as each one placed a hand gently on Nick's Arrow's neck.

"Look at those eyes," said Elaine. "They're black as coal, staring at us, almost as if she knows who we are and why we're here, like she's saying, *and You'll be proud of me.* "You're always the romantic," Maggie said.

"OK, everyone, let's leave Billy and Eddie to get ready. Nick's Arrow is running in the fifth race in post number eight."

Back In Conrad's VIP room, everyone was enjoying the beautiful day talking and drinking. They looked over the racing form to see about betting on the first four races while waiting for the fifth race.

Regina, looking at the racing form with Theresa, whispered, "I wish both Papa and Mama could be here to see this. I'm glad you decided to come with us. Let's bet. What do you think?"

"I pick by the names I like," Theresa said, giggling.

"Me too," said Regina. "You pick. I'll have the runner place the bet. Charlie, Elaine, Maggie, c'mon, Sully. You all can pick a horse; I'll put the bet in for you. If you are look at the racing form, it gives you information about the horse, jockey, and some statistics. Look at the tote board. That will tell you the calculating payoff odds if a horse should win."

CHAPTER 108

THE TIME HAD finally arrived, and the excitement escalated in the VIP room. You could hear toes tapping, the rustling movement of those shifting in their seats, photographers changing flashbulbs, and a waiter dropping a dish on the floor.

"OK, everyone, this is why you're here," Conrad said. "Watch the tote board. It's going to change rapidly since Nick's Arrow is a long shot. The announcer will be starting soon. Good luck, everyone."

"Why did he say Nick's Arrow is called a long shot?" Elaine asked.

"Nick's Arrow is new and hasn't been in a professional race," Conrad said. "This is her debut. The odds of her winning her first race are low, so it's called a long shot that she will win. Look, look! The board is saying that she is going off at fifty to one. So for every one dollar you bet on her, if she wins, you will win fifty. OK, everyone give your bets to the runners to place. Quickly now."

Regina asked the waiter to bring more champagne to the table.

"We're almost ready for the fifth race, ladies and gentlemen," the announcer said. "The betting windows are still open to place your bets. It's a brisk day here in Yonkers. The horses have been going against the wind all day. This track is one and a quarter miles, which equals ten furlongs. Here is the lineup for the fifth race…"

He continued, calling the numbers and names of the horses:

"Number 1, No It Awl.

"Number 2, Dilly Dally.

"Number 3, Rick's Rant.

"Number 4, Copper Penny.

"Number 5, Lola's Always Right.

"Number 6, Songbird.

"Number 7, Sally's Bonnet.

"Number 8, Nick's Arrow."

The trumpet started to blow with its traditional call to attention for the beginning of race five.

"Ladies and gentlemen, here at City Central Racetrack, this is a featured race since we have a new pony racing today, Nick's Arrow. She is a beauty

"Thousands of horses try to make the long journey to get here today, but only a few are chosen. Hundreds are crowding the racetrack to view the top horse in each race and to place their hopes on winning. I just received word that the betting windows are now closed.

"All the horses are in the gates. No, it seems Sally's Bonnet doesn't want to get in the gate today. Maybe she's fussing over the flowered hat that's on her head. All right, she's in, and the gate is finally closed behind her. They look ready now."

The bell rang, and the gates opened.

"And they're away," the announcer said. "It's a good start out of the gate. Copper Penny takes the lead from the number four position on the outside. The newcomer here today, Nick's Arrow, owned by Pell Global Group, is in the number-eight position, bringing this filly on the outside. They are rounding the first turn in this mile-and-a-quarter race.

"Dilly Dally and Rick's Rant are running together nose to nose, followed by Sally's Bonnet. Our newcomer, Nick's Arrow, isn't shooting too straight at the moment in fourth place.

"Dropping way behind is Songbird, whose owners aren't singing now. Here comes No It Awl from the outside, making his way to fifth place.

"Look at how strong Lola's Always Right is from the inside, coming in from the number-five gate. She's making her way past Sally's Bonnet, past Rick's Rant, who dropped behind Dilly Dally, closing the gap at the half-mile marker.

"Foot by foot, length by length, inch by inch, they're fighting as they round the last turn into the home stretch in this ten-furlong race.

"These ponies are ripping up the dirt on this mile-and-a-quarter track. Nick's Arrow has one of the best jockeys in racing, Eddie Hudson, who knows how to win as this filly comes up strong alongside Lola's Always Right and No It Awl.

"It's almost over, folks. It's Lola's Always Right, Copper Penny, No It Awl, and Nick's Arrow.

"What a jockey that Eddie Hudson is, bringing in that filly, Nick's Arrow, in fourth place. What a start for this magnificent-looking racehorse. I see great potential here, particularly if Eddie Hudson keeps riding her.

"Here it is, ladies and gentleman, the last length heading to the finish line.

"It's over, folks. First place is Lola's Always Right, paying four to one. Second place is Copper Penny, paying two to one. Third place, No It Awl, paying six to one.

"That is some performance by Eddie Hudson and the new filly, Nick's Arrow, in her first professional race, coming in fourth place. She is going to be a big moneymaker for Pell Global Group. These other three thoroughbreds are not new to this track. No It Awl does seem to know it all as he struts past, bobbing his head in confidence. Lola's Always Right wants to be right as she pushes her way through to the winner's circle, while Copper Penny is making her way to the exit. As we wait for the next race, folks, why not get yourself some refreshments at our newly decorated cafeteria located on the lower level."

CHAPTER 109

As THE STORY goes, during Elaine's early school years, before attending Bronx School of Law and Finance, a two-bit punk, Julio, thought he was the neighborhood gigolo despite his unwashed hair and thick-lensed glasses. He would go to the school dance sponsored by Saint Gregorio Church every year. Since Julio, Elaine, and Maggie went to this parochial school, they also attended this dance. Julio tried to dance with as many girls as possible. He knew through lockerroom talk what girls were easy and what girls would go all the way, as he eventually experienced with a couple of them. Julio had never heard anything about Elaine or Maggie, so he'd started by asking for a dance with Elaine, which she thought was harmless. She knew Julio from some classes they were in together, but she'd never given him a thought.

"This is so stupid," Julio said to Elaine as they were dancing. "It should be against the law to force us to go to a dance."

"Yeah, and force us to go to confession every Saturday in preparation for Sunday Mass communion," Elaine said.

"I can't wait to get out of here," Julio said.

"Yes, I'm just waiting a little while longer, and I'm going to leave too."

The dance was sort of a "had to attend," created by the priests and nuns as part of their curriculum to teach social skills. Maggie had not been feeling well and did not attend that year. She would have to submit to the reprimands for not attending and without an excuse that the school thought acceptable (which weren't many), she would take a hit on her class average. Elaine's plan was to arrive, be seen, have a few dances, make some conversation with the clergy and Sister Rachel Louise, then, having made her appearance, leave.

Julio saw her talking to those she needed to before making her getaway, getting edgy as she made her way to the door. He asked if she needed a ride home, since he had his mother's car and would be going to Allerton Avenue, supposedly, to a party some friends were having. Elaine thought nothing of it and agreed since she wanted to get home early, as her father had demanded. Once in the car a few blocks away, Julio had pulled over to the curb and leaned over to try to kiss Elaine.

"Stop it! I'm not interested. I have a boyfriend."

Julio was not satisfied with that. "Don't give me that shit. I've heard about you." He proceeded to force himself on her, almost succeeding to the point of ripping her bra and a couple of buttons.

"C'mon, Elaine. I heard about you putting out! Give a little." Julio took a chance it might be true, even as Elaine pushed him away.

"Fuck you, you stupid prick!" Elaine said in between pushing him away and trying to get the door handle opened.

"Oh, you do want my prick?" Julio stammered in a high-pitched, confrontational voice.

Elaine, in a panic and with adrenaline pumping, put up a strong defense, punching wildly enough to break his glasses and used them to stab him in the cheek, which quickly drew blood. She used the opportunity to jump out of the car right on the corner of the Third Avenue, running up the stairs to get the train home.

"You stupid cunt," Julio yelled out the window. "I'll get you for this."

Charlie never knew this until his last year at Boston University. Once he did find out, his thought was, *this stupid fuck has to learn a lesson.*

CHAPTER 110

THE SEASONS TURNED one after the other. Mama passed away over the summer, and Charlie had to make a quick trip home from his summer courses for the funeral.

Mama was laid to rest with Papa Cappelli in Woodlawn Cemetery. It was a quiet ceremony. Regina and her sisters did not want to go through what the family had to endure when Papa died, with long, drawn-out days of viewing the body with so many people coming and going.

Mama's sister, Luisa, said she could not come to America to see her sister lying in a coffin. Rather, she wanted to remember her when they were visiting together on her trip to Italy.

CHAPTER 111

IT WAS ON their last winter break from school in 1942, before graduating that upcoming summer of 1943, that both Charlie and Elaine came to grips with the reality of not letting the thing with Julio lie. They both knew there could be consequences, but they just wanted the sweetness of making the little fuck sorry for what he'd done to Elaine. Rumor had it that he'd tried the same thing with many young girls in the neighborhood and was still getting away with it. The girls were too afraid to come forward because Julio was making a reputation for himself as a local wise guy. The reality was, he only projected this image. He had no friends. He was a "fucking ingrate loser," as Charlie would often say of Julio, who was still living at home. He'd tried to join the army, but they rejected him because of his eyesight.

Charlie knew he could count on Elaine, and Elaine knew she wanted this taken care of without letting any more time slip by. She would often mutter, "I want him fucking dead!"

Charlie finally understood Elaine's wish and was 100 percent willing to help it happen. He rarely thought of the night with his cousin Benny and the murder he'd helped perpetrate.

Charlie also knew he could count on Sully, who was staying with Charlie for winter break. Charlie found out where Julio hung out with the help of Vince, who was sworn to secrecy never to tell Charlie's father why he needed this information.

Julio's hangout was a little coffee shop where Julio worked the counter, serving espresso and hard cakes to the locals who frequented played cards and dominoes in the shop. Julio would tell people who did not know the coffee shop that he owned the place. The real owners were rarely there and had a distant relative of Julio's running the joint who didn't mind Julio telling everyone he owned it.

Charlie suggested Elaine go into the shop early one morning to sit and have an espresso and a dry cake. Almost six years had passed, but Julio recognized Elaine immediately. When Elaine entered the café, Julio scurried to her table to take her order. Elaine pretended not to recognize the piece of shit, and Julio was nervous, wondering why she was there. Julio thought Elaine did not recognize him, and he politely and charmingly started to talk to her. *She doesn't know who I am*, he thought. *I'll get even with this bitch.*

"Hi, I'm known as Rosario. Do you need to see the menu?" Julio said as he squinted without his glasses.

Elaine thought, *Rosario, you dirty motherfucker. Now you really will feel the pain that's coming.* "No, I'll just have espresso and a cake." Julio ran to the back to get the order himself while his aunt took care of the other customers.

Julio returned with Elaine's order. "Zucchero?"

"Yes, sugar, no cream," Elaine said.

"I haven't seen you around here," he said, trying to be sure she didn't recognize him.

"I'm visiting and doing some shopping on Fordham Road."

"You know, I know the area very well and can tell you where to get great bargains and what stores to stay away from."

"That would be great. Can you tell me now? Come. Sit. I mean, can you?"

"Yes, just give me a moment."

This piece of shit really thinks he's going to get a second chance by fooling me with his greasy hair and horrible, cheap-smelling cologne, Elaine thought.

When Julio returned, he had taken off his apron, hanging it across his shoulder. He was carrying two fresh espressos and another cake for Elaine.

"So, who are you visiting and what do you need to shop for?" he asked, placing the espresso in front of her. "I'm sorry. I told you my name, what's yours?"

"Elaine. Is this your place?"

"Oh yes. I've owned it for six or seven years. That's my Aunt Melissa working over there."

"So, I'm shopping for my sister's wedding," Elaine lied. "Well, really a gift for her bridal shower."

"You know, I can take you to dinner and have a list of stores where you can get a great bargain. How can I call you?"

"You can't," Elaine snapped. "I mean, I'll meet you. Do you know—of course you do—187th and Southern Boulevard? I'll meet you there at six thirty Friday evening. Is that good for you?"

Immediately Julio thought, *That is going to be a good night for me. She is beautiful.*

"Yes, of course. There's a place only two blocks from there that has great spaghetti and calamari. There's a little newsstand there if it gets too cold for you to wait outside. I'll find you. See you then. I've got to get back to the counter." He put his apron back on. "The espresso and cake is on me. Enjoy. *Ciao.*"

CHAPTER 112

ELAINE TOLD CHARLIE about her "date" with Julio.

Unfortunately, Sully couldn't go with Charlie as promised. He had to leave to be home since his mother's illness was getting worse.

"Don't concern yourself," Charlie assured Sully. "Your mother is more important."

Charlie picked Elaine up at her house about five thirty, giving them enough time to drive around the spot Julio was going to meet Elaine, scoping out what they were going to do and how they were going to do it.

Sunlight was fading fast as they drove the area, finding where the newsstand and the restaurant were located.

"Look," Charlie said. "This can be a good thing here. I found out from... never mind, about this icehouse. See it right there? There's a security guard who goes for coffee every evening at the same time and sets out a brick to hold the door open because he's supposed to stay inside all night. He's been doing it for years. He's old, fat, and drinks. We have about fifteen minutes before this shithead gets here." Charlie pulled into a parking space directly across from the newsstand. Lowering the heater, he leaned in to kiss Elaine. "Are you OK with this?"

"Am I OK with what, you kissing me or fucking him up?"

Laughing, Charlie said, "Fucking this douchebag up a lot or a little?"

"As much as I can," she said, grabbing him and putting her tongue in his mouth. "I want to continue this after. I've missed you. I want you."

"I love you," Charlie said.

"And I love you. Oh shit! He's here. Look, over there. He's parking his car. It's the same car from that night. What a stupid fuck!"

"OK," Charlie said. "Wait for him to get out. He's probably going in the newsstand to see if you're there. He'll probably want to drive to the restaurant. Let him go into the newsstand. Then you start to walk over. He'll come out and see you walking. When he starts to take you to his car, tell him you dropped an earring and want to look for it, bringing him toward that ramp of the icehouse. Pretend you don't find it; then tell him you'd rather walk to the restaurant since it's only a block or two. We have to time this perfectly, Elaine. The security guard goes for coffee at eight o'clock. You have to finish dinner and be back here at five minutes past eight. If you have to, tell him you feel ill. Walk him back toward that ramp and say the earrings were a gift from your grandmother, and you want to look again for it. Go, he just walked in. I'll be circling the block. Don't worry. Take one of your earrings off, quickly."

CHAPTER 113

"Ah, there you are," Julio said, coming out of the newsstand. "I thought for a second you'd backed out."

"You really didn't have to take me to dinner, Rosario. You could have just given me a list of stores you were telling me about," Elaine said to Julio, playing his game.

"Yeah, I know, but I wanted to see you again and maybe get to know each other, and who knows."

"Huh? Who knows what?"

"Here's my car. I'll drive."

"I'd rather walk; you said the restaurant is only a block or two."

As they walked, Julio kept blowing into his hands, rubbing them together for warmth, since he didn't have any gloves. They said very little to each other, just mundane talk about the weather, the city garbage trucks, and part of the Bronx Zoo across the street.

"Here we are," Julio said happily, holding the door open.

After she was seated, Elaine asked, "What were you saying back there?"

"Nothing. Let's order," said Julio, removing his glasses, which had fogged after coming into the warmth of the restaurant from the outside cold air.

"I'm not feeling that well, and I lost an earring while I was waiting for you," Elaine said. "I'll just have a soup, Minestrone."

"The same for me," Julio said, thinking, *I hope she doesn't have her period.*

The small talk continued, with Julio bragging about his café and the people he knew and how he did "this and that," while Elaine kept looking at her watch.

"This soup is good," she said, sipping from her spoon.

"You keep looking at your watch. Do you have to be somewhere? I thought we could take a drive after dinner and—"

Elaine interrupted him. "I'm really not feeling good. I'm sorry, Rosario. I have that earring on my mind. My grandmother gave it to me, and I heard it drop. Can we go back and look after we finish our soup? Maybe you have a flashlight in your car? And don't forget the list of stores you told me about."

"I'll give it to you now. I hope you can read my handwriting," Julio answered almost with a snarl as he handed Elaine a folded piece of paper, glancing up through his thick glasses to be sure Elaine was missing an earring.

"Thank you, Rosario. I'm sorry. Maybe we can do this again. I'll stop by your café, I promise," Elaine said, playing the game.

As soon as they finished their soup, Julio plopped down money on the table and helped Elaine with her coat. He was obviously disappointed and rejected, hardly finding words on the walk back.

Elaine saw Charlie pass them in his car, knowing they were going back to where they started. He accelerated past them to go park and wait. As they approached, Charlie was wondering why they were going to Julio's car. *No, no. What are you doing?*

Julio opened the door and reached into the glove box for a flashlight. Both Julio and Elaine started to walk toward the ramp of the icehouse just as the security guard passed them to go the newsstand for his coffee. Julio turned the flashlight. When it didn't light, he pounded it into the palm of his hand, hoping it would shake the batteries to their senses in his time of need.

"Works every time," Julio said proudly as a dim glow appeared.

"It was more over here that I heard it drop. Shine it here," Elaine demanded.

Charlie quietly approached Julio from behind, encircling Julio's neck with a nylon rope and squeezing it tightly as he had seen Benny do in Italy. Julio dropped the flashlight, which Elaine immediately picked up. Julio squirmed, frantically trying to free himself, trying to get his hands between the rope and his neck. He gasped for air as Charlie dragged him toward the door the security guard had left ajar.

"Hurry, hold the door open," commanded Charlie, continuing to drag Julio, who was getting weaker. Charlie, not knowing where he was going, dragged him through a second door, which opened to a room filled with blocks of ice. It was freezing. Julio was gagging as he struggled less and less.

Elaine looked Julio in the eyes as they began to bulge.

"You tried to rape me like you raped other girls," she said. "Not anymore."

Looking around, Elaine saw tools for cutting the ice blocks—chisels saws, grapples, and tongs. She picked up an icepick, raised it over her head, and plunged it into his chest as easily as it would cut into a thick block of ice. Blood started coming through Julio's coat in spurts, like an oil well. Charlie and Elaine watched the gush of blood that quickly ended the meeting. Charlie let go, dropping Julio to the floor. Julio laid face up, his eyes gray and empty, just like the cloudy blocks of ice.

"Get the flashlight," said Elaine. "What's that smell?"

"No, leave it," Charlie said, dropping the nylon rope on the floor.

The question Elaine asked and the smell immediately sparked Charlie's memory of the night with Benny in Italy at the watershed.

"He shit his pants. Let's go. Shh. Quiet."

"That's disgusting."

They pushed the exit door open slowly to be sure no one was passing. They had plenty of time before the security guard returned, according to the information Charlie was able to get. After placing the brick exactly where it had been, they scurried down the ramp. Cold air hit them in the face, causing them to see their own breath as they exhaled. Crossing the street to Charlie's parked car, they immediately embraced and a deep loving kiss, their passion fogging the windows.

Pulling away from Elaine and immediately starting the car, Charlie said, "We need to go. We can never talk about this, even to each other as of now. *Never!* Do you understand?" He spoke in a commanding tone.

"My parents are in Long Island at my grandmother's for the night," Elaine said. "Take me home. I want you to fuck me."

CHAPTER 114

THE WORLD WAS in turmoil. War in Europe was causing havoc. Charlie's letters to Benny and Sophia showed much concern. However, he received fewer letters in response. Some of their last writings explained that Italy was participating in the war.

Ever since Mussolini had begun to falter, Hitler had been making plans to invade Italy to keep the Allies from gaining a foothold that would situate them within easy reach of the German-occupied Balkans. Hitler launched Operation Axis, the occupation of Italy. As German troops entered Rome, General Badoglio and the royal family fled Rome for southeastern Italy to set up a new anti-Fascist government. Italian troops began surrendering to their former German allies.

The Adonis Winery had to focus on how to save the wine from destruction, since Italy had surrendered to Germany and was occupied. The last letter Charlie received from Sophia was as if she had a bad dream about what to do with the wine, but it was real and not a dream. It was just as real as the war and just as real when the German tanks rolled with thunderous energy into the small towns after occupying Rome.

"We are shipping hundreds of wooden cases stuffed with straw to protect the wine bottles to the hills and farms in Switzerland to have a supply if and when this stupid fucking thing ever ends."

Less and less was sent to the United States, although it was one of the last outlets to receive stock from Adonis Winery before production came to a complete stop.

The United States had been thrust into the war for over a year, and life on the home front had changed drastically, including the horse-racing world. The lack of jockeys and other track workers because of military service or work in defense plants, coupled with rationing, was taking its toll.

Nick's Arrow was now on a farm in Kentucky being cared for and groomed by her trainer, Billy Jackson. However, the expenses still remained, so it was one investment that had no return for Pell Global Group.

"Fortunately," Regina would often say, "we don't have to worry. I pray to Saint Christopher.[1] He is always with us. He covers all that we do."

Charlie, overhearing his mother many times saying; *Saint Christopher is always with us is now asking himself; Can Saint Christopher cover what we did to Julio and the itinerant drunk in Italy. Why would he?*

It was true. Michael, Regina, and the family were wealthy beyond imagination. Very few things changed in their life.

They never had to participate in the rationing that was taking place. The Pell Global Group was still supplying the government with apples at only two cents above cost and expenses, and the government was quite indebted to them, giving special dispensation for their fleet of trucks and whatever else they needed. Regina would take whatever rations she could and distribute them to many who were without.

---

1 Saint Christopher is invoked against pestilence, ailments, dangers, and transportation.

CHAPTER 115

ALTHOUGH THE PELLS had crossed many hurdles over the years, they were having some of their best moments with their son. Not only was he able to go past eighth grade, the highest education anyone in either family had accomplished, he was also in the 1943 graduating class of one of the most prestigious colleges in the country, Boston University.

Charlie's father invited friends, relatives, and local politicians to a party for Charlie and his best friend, Sully, who graduated the same year as Charlie. The guest list included politicians from Washington, DC, such as Congressman Fineman, Federal Judge Anthony Neopali, Bronx County District Attorney Richards, as well as Chief of Police Jerry Houlihan, New York City Mayor Edward Miley, Senator Silver, and Governor Roberts, just to mention a few dignitaries. These were all powerhouses who carried a lot of clout in many parts of the country, not just New York. The list was enormous. He even included some of his friends from Grace Bar and Grill. Michael wanted every one of his contacts to meet the next generation they would have to deal with.

The event was being held at the Island Casino right on the water. You could walk out to the elegant patio or stroll on the private beach. It was a perfect summer night with a sea breeze that salted the air. The women wore dazzling dresses with high-heeled shoes. Regina's dressmaker, Tabitha, outdid herself, creating a silver sequined dress that magnificently outlined her exquisite form. The gentleman wore tailored suits with shoes shined so well they could see their reflections.

Regina, with the help of Theresa, hired an orchestra with violins, trumpets, saxophones, drums, piano, and a famous singer—Bobby Valentine.

Bobby Valentine had grown up on the Bronx streets, fought some Golden Gloves boxing matches. He didn't want to get his face pummeled and his brains smashed. He was a man's man. Not only did the women want to sleep with him, but the men wanted to hang around with him. He had a charisma no one could imitate. It just flowed out of him like the lyrics of a song in his velvet voice.

Bobby always had a soft spot for boxers and would do some benefit shows to help the ones who were down-and-out. His two bodyguards were ex-boxers, and both knew Michael's friend Joey Adams. Bobby left an engagement at the Fountain Hotel in Miami Beach, Florida, and flew right into New York with his music arranger, Marshall Stein, to be at Charlie's graduation party. Bobby Valentine owed Michael a favor. Bobby's Hollywood agent, Jimmy Cohen, was a friend of Michael's and with Bill Sullivan's encouragement, was able to help Jimmy negotiate a union movie deal for Bobby with one of the head honchos at Midway Studios.

It was going to be Bobby's first shot at the silver screen. His part called for a truck driver who wanted to become a singer and eventually made it to Broadway. Right after the party, he had to fly to California for acting lessons that Michael and Jimmy Cohen had arranged.

Bobby and his wife and son were going to relocate to Palms Boulevard, Culver City, California, which was just a short drive to Midway Studios and the heart of Hollywood. The house was a nice ranch home with three bedrooms, a swimming pool, and a large lawn and patio for parties, which Bobby would have to host now that he was in Hollywood, all arranged by Pell Global Group. Regina, Theresa, and Gina Ponti had a special hand in arranging this move. They often flew to California to meet with Bobby's wife, Patti.

Elaine came up to Charlie and asked him to dance as soon as the orchestra started to play.

"I didn't know your father knew Bobby Valentine," Elaine whispered.

"These are only a handful of important people we will soon know too."

Elaine crunched her eyebrows together as she snuggled closer into Charlie's shoulder, understanding exactly what he meant by *we will soon know too.*

The music stopped. Charlie walked Elaine to her table and sought out Maggie, who was talking to Bobby Valentine's music arranger, Marshall Stein, to see how to further her music career.

Deep in conversation, Marshall told Maggie, "When you finish your studies, get in touch with me. If you are good enough to be first violinist, as you say you're going to be, there can always be a place for you doing movie music scores."

Maggie looked dazed at the man, who only stood a little over five feet, neatly appointed in his tailor-made double-breasted suit. Charlie heard Maggie saying, "Yes, thank you, thank you. I will, I will."

"Maggie, you all right?" Charlie asked.

"Oh yes," she said, almost skipping past Charlie. "This is wonderful, wonderful, thank you," she said as she continued on past him.

Bill Sullivan was grateful to Michael for including his son, Sully, in this bash, even having Sully's name listed on the program. It meant a lot to Bill, who had not been himself since his wife, Mary, had died last year.

Elaine was continuing on to finish law school at Fordham University, contemplating criminal law.

At different intervals, Michael and Regina would take Charlie with them and work the room, introducing him to everyone who held a prominent position. Charlie was gracious, shaking hands and making small talk, then moving on to more and more introductions:

"Charlie, this is…"

"Charlie, this is…"

"Charlie, this is…"

"Charlie, this is…"

"Charlie, this is…" until he could not keep track of who was whom. He sought out Elaine for another dance.

Catching Elaine's eye, Charlie excused himself to walk toward her as she extended her arm. The orchestra was playing a slow song.

"Hey, Mr. Popular, do you have time for me?" Elaine asked.

"Don't even ask. Only you."

The band stopped playing when the conductor gave the signal after being handed a note. He turned to the audience and stepped to the microphone.

"Let me have your attention, ladies and gentlemen. I was just handed this note by Senator Silver that reads, 'US Navy warplanes and warships conclude their bombardment of Japanese positions, pushing them all the way back to their starting point, killing hundreds of the enemy.'"

The applause and yelps of cheer became deafening. Some of the guests had lost loved ones to the war: sons, daughters, brothers, nephews, and fathers. Women removed their hankies, wiping away tears of joy and sorrow.

Bobby Valentine quickly jumped to the stage and whispered to the conductor, who struck up the orchestra. Bobby started to sing "As Time Goes By" in his velvet voice.

You must remember this
A kiss is still a kiss
A sigh is still a sigh
As time goes by

Everyone began dancing; every seat in the house was empty. If there wasn't a man to dance with, the ladies danced with each other.

"I want this to be our song," Elaine whispered to Charlie, continuing to sing along to the lyrics in his ear.

And when two lovers woo, they still say I love you...

"I love you, Charlie," Elaine said.

The fundamental things apply
as time goes by

"C'mon, let's go out to the beach and make love on one of the chaise lounges."

Charlie took Elaine by the hand, leading her out through the French doors to the patio along the walkway to the beach, where they would make love out in the open. Charlie's manhood began to swell just thinking about Elaine's beauty. *After the murder with Benny in Italy, I couldn't wait to go with Sophia, and I was so absorbed in fucking her. Both Elaine and myself, after the heavyweight fight and then after doing Julio in, couldn't wait to get to her house and fuck, and we did it until dawn. And now Elaine, after hearing how hundreds of Japanese enemy were killed, wants to make love again. Me too! We're meant to be...*

Just at that moment, Elaine guided Charlie on top of her, lifting her dress. He found she wasn't wearing any panties as he plunged into her like a runaway freight train with no conductor.

CHAPTER 116

ELAINE FINISHED HER law school with a juris doctor from Fordham Law University. She passed her bar exam easily, keeping focused on what she wanted to accomplish, which was to be part of the Pell family, love Charlie forever, and be a kick-ass lawyer.

Charlie, already working with Pell Global Group from his own office in Manhattan, was quickly beginning to realize the enormity of wealth and ownership he was part of now. There were meetings to attend with many individuals of prominence, and then there are meetings of the inner circle: his father, Izzy, Bill Sullivan, and Vince. When Regina attended, it was mostly about bookkeeping and costs and profits from all their holdings.

Charlie would always listen intently, often holding off before voicing an opinion or suggestion. Once he came up with a cost-savings solution to have distribution warehouses strategically located, so their trucks would travel shorter distances, saving thousands in fuel. The added cost of the buildings would be a write-off, at the same time adding value to their real estate holdings. He also set up each distribution center to operate on its own merit. Each manager would have to show a profit and in turn would earn a bonus.

Elaine met Charlie for lunch. They went to his favorite lunch place, Empire Deli. Elaine and Charlie passed his father's office, and Charlie poked his head in to tell him where he and Elaine were going. Both Michael and Regina were always happy to see Elaine, greeting her with the traditional kiss on each cheek.

"Before you go, I want to ask you something, Elaine," Michael said. "Regina, Theresa, Horace Worthington, and Bill Sullivan are going to California to negotiate another movie deal for Bobby Valentine. His first movie didn't go over so well, and we need some hard negotiating. Charlie tells me you are one hell of a lawyer. Since you haven't made a decision as to where you're going to work, I'd like to make you an offer to travel with them and sit in on the negotiations, maybe consider working here at Pell Global Group. Go to lunch and think about it."

Elaine, smiling brightly, said, "Absolutely, Mr. Pell. I don't have to think about it. You can count on me. I'm definitely in. Thank you."

"You need to call me Michael."

"Yes, it is time for not being formal," Regina said. "That goes for me too."

"Charlie's very lucky to have you both," Elaine said. "Would you like to join us for lunch?"

"No, go and enjoy," Regina said. "I'm sure you have a lot to talk about. Be sure to take one of the detectives with you."

"I don't want to do that unless it's absolutely a necessity," Charlie said.

Elaine gently patted Charlie on his chest. "It's OK, Charlie." Turning to Regina, she added, "We will."

After they left his office, Michael said, "She reminds me of you. I bet she's going to be around a long time."

Arriving at Empire Deli, they were greeted by Boris. "Ah, Charlie, it's good to see you. You've grown up too fast."

"Thank you, Boris. Elaine, this is Boris Glicksman, the owner. Boris, this is Elaine Solofra."

"Pleased to meet you, Elaine. Charlie, you have a winner here," said Boris with a big smile, shaking Elaine's hand vigorously. Boris snapped his finger for the waiter to attend to the table.

"Oh, the singing waiters…This should be fun!" said Elaine.

CHAPTER 117

MICHAEL CALLED A meeting in their private room with his inner circle.

"Great unprecedented news. I just received a call from Conrad. Sam is in his seventh year of his eight-year term as governor. Because of the lingering war and the great job he's doing as governor, the people don't want change and have passed a temporary law to extend his term another four years. So it seems we have a five-year window to prep him and do whatever we have to do to get him the presidency. We can't fuck this up. We need to start now thinking about the campaign and how to present him to the public, which should be simple, since he is loved by the people. This is going to take a lot of work and a lot of our contacts. I hope this war ends soon so we can bring our boys home.

"Izzy, pack your bags. I need you and Adele to head to Miami. Conrad also told me that the Colony Hotel is in trouble and may have to go up for sale. They won't know who you are, so you can go as tourists. You know what to look for. Adele is an asset. Use her to her best ability to get information. We'll need all the ammunition we can muster to squeeze them...Go." He waved his hand to shoo him out. "Speak to Theresa. She'll make your arrangements."

"We'll stay and have a nice visit," Izzy said. "Adele will love it just like she loved Cuba. Too bad Fats isn't around." Michael and Bill nodded in agreement, grimacing.

"Vince," Michael continued, "I need you here with me and Charlie. I have Bill, Horace, Regina, and Theresa, plus Charlie's girlfriend, Elaine, who also is an attorney, going to California for Valentine's new movie deal and house decorating with Patty. I want you to take Charlie to Grace Bar and Grill and introduce him to Anna Charme and some of the girls. Wait for Regina to leave for California with everyone else."

Vince chuckled. "It's been a while since I've visited there. Do you want me to bring Anna a gift as usual?"

"As usual. Be sure this envelope is really fat. I have a feeling we're going to be seeing Anna often over the next few years. She's gathering some important information for us."

CHAPTER 118

Izzy and Adele arrived at Miami's airport, where a chauffeured limousine waited for them. The skycap retrieved their luggage.

"I like Miami," said Adele in her high-pitched voice. "The sun shines all the time. I always feel different, like when we used to go to Cuba."

"You got sick, really bad, a few times when we were in Cuba," Izzy said. "What, all of a sudden, you have amnesia? We couldn't even fuck after a few days."

"Theresa does a good job doing all these arrangements," Adele went on, ignoring Izzy's remark. "I couldn't do it."

It was a short limousine ride before the car pulled up in front of the Colony Hotel on South Flagler Drive, just steps from the ocean in the heart of Miami Beach, the new mecca for grown-ups to play and have fun in the sun. It was certainly a tasteful place with people of taste. Celebrities flocked to the location for quick getaways where no one hounded them for autographs or pictures.

Adele looked out the window. "This is really beautiful, Izzy. Look at that building. It almost looks like the Empire State Building. I never saw buildings painted different colors except in Cuba. I love the pink and blue."

As they entered the lobby, exquisite marble floors and walls reflected their image. Color lighting created an atmosphere that helped change your mind-set and mood to one of "put all your cares and woes away; enjoy your life to the fullest."

Izzy and Adele approached the check-in manager, who welcomed them.

"Thank you for choosing the Colony Hotel, the Pink Jewel of Miami Beach, Mr. and Mrs. Solomon. We're here to fulfill your request. Your New York office has everything in order." He rang the bell for the bellhop to gather their luggage and escort them to their room.

CHAPTER 119

Izzy and Adele were escorted to their room, which opened to a stunning view of the ocean, its waves gently rolling onto the glistening sand. Their room was simple and elegant, just one bedroom and a living room sitting area. The hotel called it a suite. The bellboy put some of the luggage on the beds and some on the luggage stand. Izzy handed him a five-dollar tip.

"Thank you, Mr. Solomon. That's very generous. Is there anything else I can get you or Mrs. Solomon?"

"Not at the moment. Tell me; is the hotel usually so quiet? I mean, this place is beautiful. I would think it would be filled."

"It depends on the time of year, Mr. Solomon. We get a lot more tourists during the winter months, when the weather is the best in the world, if you ask me. The summer gets really hot if you're not used to it. You have to be careful of the sun any time of year, even on a cloudy day. It will bite you. You know, it's the tropics. The rest of the year it fluctuates."

"Thanks, that's all."

Adele called to Izzy, "Look at this bathroom. I love the colors—pink, black, and white."

"The only thing pink I'm interested in right now is those beautiful tits of yours."

"You mean these," Adele said, teasingly unbuttoning her blouse and removing her brassiere.

CHAPTER 120

IZZY AND ADELE lay on the beach in lounge chairs, enjoying the turquoise color of the ocean. After having lunch and drinks served to them, they headed back to the pool for more booze and lounging. Izzy was always asking questions of the help. Adele helped by being flirtatious, both of them digging for answers about the operations of the exquisite one-hundred-fifty-room hotel. During supper, which included cocktails and fresh fish, they took their time exploiting the help, who came to the table one by one.

Adele looked around.

"Why does that table keep staring at us?" she whispered to Izzy. "It's making me feel uncomfortable."

"Who? I don't see them staring. I can go over to them."

"No, it's OK. Eat. Don't worry about it."

Dinner wasn't finished when Adele told Izzy, "I'm not feeling too good tonight. I have cramps and a terrible pain in my abdomen. I need to go upstairs." Izzy helped her off her chair and had Adele lean on him when they walked together. They gave the appearance of drinking too much as they swayed from side to side.

"Maybe it's too much booze and sun," Izzy said. "Let's get you to bed."

"Yes, I'm sorry. I need to go to sleep."

CHAPTER 121

THE NEXT FEW days were touch and go with Adele. She was always tired or feeling sick to her stomach and had to go to their room to sleep. Izzy would take advantage of this time to roam the hotel for information. Using his charm and wit, he was able to take a personal tour of the hotel, saying he was in the restaurant business back in New York and would love to see how such a huge operation ran so smoothly. He got the night manager to personally escort him all around the entire hotel, including the kitchen, where he watched the executive chef in full operation.

Getting back to the room, Izzy saw Adele hadn't finished her drink or her cigarette, which was burning in the ashtray. She seemed to have taken a sedative to help her sleep, an ordinary occurrence with her. Then he realized what was in the wastebasket next to the bed. She had thrown up!

He touched her skin in some areas that were dark and swollen. Immediately he grabbed the phone to dial the desk, ordering the clerk to get an ambulance.

CHAPTER 122

Izzy was pacing outside Adele's room, waiting for the doctors to finish with their exam, while he puffed on a cigarette.

"You can't smoke here," a nurse screamed out. "There are oxygen tanks in the rooms. Put it out *now*!"

"Where?" Izzy asked, almost in a panic, not seeing a receptacle.

"On the floor. Now! I'll get it cleaned up."

The two doctors and nurse left Adele's room, bringing them face-to-face with Izzy.

"So, what is going on with my wife?" Izzy asked.

"We actually don't know, Mr. Solomon," one of the doctors said. "We haven't seen something like this. We have to monitor her and continue with some testing. She is sedated now. You can go in and stay with her."

Izzy almost broke the door down to get in. Standing over her, he held her hand and started to rub her forehead. He pushed her hair away from her eyes, bending to gently kiss her.

Adele started to awaken at about three that morning. Moaning softly, she rolled her head side to side, trying to open her eyes.

"Izzy, is that you?" she called out, feeling disoriented.

Izzy quickly jumped from the chair he had fallen asleep in, throwing the blanket one of the nurses had covered him with on the floor.

"Yes, yes, it's me. How are you doing?"

"Where am I? What the fuck happened to me?"

"When I came to the room, you were passed out. You'd thrown up and left a cigarette burning. Your skin was all fucked up. I called an ambulance. You're in the hospital."

"I don't want to stay here. I feel better. Let's go back to the hotel and pack and go home." She tried to swing her legs off the side of the bed to stand but collapsed in Izzy's arms.

"It's OK. The doctor said the sedative will take the night to wear off. Let's get you back in the bed for now." Izzy gently placed her back on the bed, saying, "I'd love to climb in there with you."

Adele barely answered him with, "C'mon," before falling into a deep sleep again.

Izzy went to the bathroom to wash his face before walking down to the nurse's station.

"Can I use the phone? I'll pay you."

"I'm not allowed," said the nurse on duty.

Izzy reached into his pocket and pulled out his money clip, peeling off a fifty-dollar bill and laying it on her desk.

Looking around to see if anyone was in the hallway, she slid the bill into the front pocket of her uniform and said, "Hurry and be quiet." She left her post to walk to the bathroom, her shoes making a squeaking noise with every step on the highlypolished floor.

CHAPTER 123

VINCE INTRODUCED CHARLIE to Anna Charme. She was enamored by the young, handsome man and his charm.

"You have your father's good looks and beautiful hazel eyes, Charlie. I would love to have you myself; however, I know you'd like a younger, newer girl. What types of women do you like—blond, redhead, or brunette? Big tits, just a handful? Tall, short? White, colored, Spanish? For you, I'll get them lined up so you can choose."

Grabbing Charlie's hand and leading him and Vince through a secret wall panel that took them to a staircase to a second level, Anna rang a bell. Suddenly there were seven beautiful young women to choose from. Charlie's eyes darted from woman to woman, all dressed in sheer, provocative negligees. Slowly, he walked past each one, stopping in front of a beautiful, long-legged, small-breasted lady with soft, beautiful, deep-olive skin.

When he took her hand, she said, "Hi, I'm Cassandra. I'm from Persia. You can call me Cassie."

Vince handed Anna a thick envelope filled with cash as he picked another beautiful woman for himself. Anna sneaked a peek into the envelope, running her thumb over the bills to get a glimpse of her gift.

"Thank you. Let Michael know I certainly will do what I've done in the past for him. Go, enjoy. OK, girls, back to the bar."

CHAPTER 124

ELAINE WAS INCREDIBLE negotiating with the studio's attorneys. The conference room was crowded. Everyone important was there: Bobby, Jimmy Cohen, Horace, Bill, Regina, Elaine, and the studio attorneys. Theresa and Gina were out with Patty Valentine looking for furniture. Elaine had reviewed the contracts on the plane.

All of Bobby Valentine's team was brought into the conference room before Midway Studios' attorneys arrived.

Elaine addressed everyone who was in the room.

"It's OK. It's a ploy." She directed each one where to sit, not leaving the other attorney's team a choice on seating. When the studio people would walk in, they would be caught off guard, since Elaine had changed the place cards with everyone's names on them. It was as if she were directing a class of children.

"Don't speak unless I ask you to talk," she directed them. Just as expected, when Midway's people entered, they realized their seating arrangements had all been adjusted. It took them a moment to find their place cards, causing them a little embarrassment.

After a few hours of back and forth and give-and-take, Elaine quoted something that Abraham Lincoln said: "'A good settlement is better than a good lawsuit.' Fair market value of a contract is determined by what the willing parties will and will not accept. We don't accept paragraphs seven, eight, nine, and ten on page thirty-nine, which you are now in breach of."

"You're correct, Mrs. Solafra," said the head studio attorney, Mr. Quinnappolis. "However, we made it up in paragraph twelve on page forty-one."

"It's Miss, Miss Solafra, and Mr. Quinnappolis, no, you didn't. Paragraphs seven, eight, nine, and ten say you will provide Mr. Valentine with paid housing and housekeeping, along with any services that would be needed in and around the home, including a child-sitting service, in addition to his studio salary. The paragraph you mention on page forty-one says that these will be deducted from his salary, in contradiction to the earlier points and breaches this contract. We also have to review Mr. Valentine's salary as stated in paragraph four on page fifty-one. We need to remove the clause that is misleading. We agreed that Mr. Valentine's salary would increase every six months for the first eighteen months, not after eight months only."

Silence befell the room. Elaine hoped her team remembered not to speak. Everyone did just as she instructed, sitting in silence.

Mr. Quinnappolis thought he was like a Greek god, so handsome and dressed just like one of the movie stars in one of Midway Studios' films. He thought he could manipulate and force feed anything to anyone at any time, including Elaine. Elaine sat silently, staring at him until he spoke.

"Oh! I see, Miss Solofra. That must have been a typographical error of eight and not eighteen," he said, trying not to show his deception. "OK, we'll make all the corrections you requested. No need to go any further, Miss Solofra, by quoting Abraham Lincoln again. You'll get what you want included in the contract and what you want taken out. It will only take us a few moments to make the changes. Can I get you or your guests anything while you wait?"

"No, thank you, Mr. Quinnappolis," she said. Everyone followed her lead, shaking their heads.

Elaine was eager to get back home, but that wouldn't happen for a few more days. The studio had planned a celebration the next evening to welcome Bobby Valentine for his new start, forgetting the last picture he starred in.

CHAPTER 125

REGINA TELEPHONED MICHAEL to tell him negotiations were over.

Michael picked up the phone at home. "Hello."

"Michael, I miss you. I can't wait to get home. Elaine is brilliant. She handled all the studio attorneys like leading sheep to slaughter, and that's just what she did. She slaughtered them, and they agreed to her terms."

"I miss you too," Michael said. "Charlie made a good choice. I hope he keeps her around."

"Midway Studios offered her a job."

"And..." Michael's lip started to twitch, and his voice sounded almost angry.

"She said, 'I already have a job. I'm with Pell Global Group,'" Regina said proudly.

"Ah! She is brilliant. I want you to know I'm seeing you lying next to me with just your see-through negligee, the red one."

"I'll be home in three days. I'm looking forward being with you too. There's a studio party for Bobby tomorrow evening, and the day after that, we finish up with the decorating of their house. Our flight is the day after that. Keep thinking red."

Click.

CHAPTER 126

REGINA ARRIVED HOME with Theresa, both exhausted from all the traveling, meetings, shopping, and cocktail parties. Regina left Theresa, the housekeepers, and the detectives to deal with emptying the limousine.

"Michael, I'm home," she cried out.

"Welcome home," Rosa said. "Mr. Pell isn't here, ma'am."

"Thank you, Miss Rosa. I'm going to take a bath. Have the luggage brought up, please."

"Yes, Miss Regina. Can I get you anything, something to eat or tea?"

"Yes, please. Terreno Rico Red wine. Bring up a small bottle. Thank you, Miss Rosa."

"Right away," Rosa said as she scurried to the pantry. "I'll put some crackers and cheese with it."

Entering her bedroom suite, Regina immediately kicked off her shoes, undoing the zipper on her dress and letting it drop to the floor. She continued walking while tugging off her silk slip. At the edge of the bed, she carefully removed her nylon stockings, leaving on her bra and panties. At the knock on the bedroom door, she reached for her robe.

"Come in, Miss Rosa. Thank you. Put it on my table next to the tub. Please start the water. Oh, crackers and cheese too. Thank you. That is thoughtful."

"You're welcome. Anything else for now?"

"No."

Once the door closed behind Rosa, Regina walked to the tub, undoing her robe to remove her bra and panties. She caught a glimpse of herself in the mirror and stopped for a moment to reflect on her own beauty and to gently rub her breasts. She watched her nipples quickly grow perky; then she stepped into the hot water and poured herself a glass of wine.

After twenty minutes the water started to cool. Regina released the drain and got out to finish her primping, finally making it to the bed with her robe untied. She set her wineglass and bottle on the night table next to the bed. As Regina opened her book, she reached over to sip her wine, but was startled by the door opening.

"Wow!" said Michael. "I'm so glad you're home."

"I'm tired and have a headache."

Leaning to give her a kiss, Michael said, "I'll shower. Can you pour me a drink? Oh, never mind. I'll get it. You mentioned your headache."

After showering, with a whiskey he poured from the bottle on the nightstand, Michael sat next to Regina. He took a sip before placing the glass down, pulling her closer.

"I'm sorry you're tired." His voice was muffled as he started to kiss her neck. "But, I think…no, I know I can help with that headache." He tickled her earlobe.

"Mmm," Regina said in a low tone. She moaned, moving her head in a circular motion, inviting more kisses.

"Here, let me rub your feet," Michael suggested. "You like that."

"Oh, that sounds as good as it's going to feel," she said with a sigh of relief.

Michael continued his hands downward to rub Regina's feet. Seeing she was almost asleep, he moved closer behind her and placed his hand under her robe, on her breast. Feeling her nipples grow, he gently rubbed them between his index finger and thumb, sending a sensation through her body. He felt her back pushing closer to his erection.

"I don't care if I'm tired and I have a headache," Regina said. "I want you inside me." She turned herself to face him.

"Take off your panties," Michael said, reaching to help.

"I'm not wearing any."

"I feel that." He placed his fingers on her clit, slowly rubbing and feeling Regina's response as she became wet.

Regina was aroused and ready for Michael to possess her. She ran her hands over his chest and back to help remove his robe, then reached for his hard cock to fill her emptiness, which was throbbing and waiting. She guided him inside her.

Michael started to thrust and roughly pulled Regina closer by her legs so he could thrust upward. He filled her vagina all the way as she stretched and arched her back, finding a good rhythm. Regina grabbed Michael's face to bring his lips closer to her, and then drove her tongue into his mouth. Regina realized his fucking was a little arrogant but didn't care. She was enjoying the pleasure it was giving her.

They were moving together as one, and Regina's pussy became tightly contracted around his penis.

"I feel you are part of me," she said. "*Non smettere!*"[1] Michael continued to ride her while moving his hand to massage her clitoris. Regina wrapped her legs tighter, squeezing as she released her vagina's energy in her orgasm, repeating breathlessly, "*Sì, sì. Cum dentro di me. Ti amo.*"[2]

At that moment, he felt his penis pulsate with each spurt inside her magnificent being.

Michael continued to hold Regina, snuggling into her breasts.

"You, know," Regina said, "my headache is gone."

"Maybe I should have become a doctor."

"Oh no!" Regina said with a big grin. "I don't want you curing anyone's headaches but mine."

---

1 Don't stop!

2 Yes, yes. Come inside me. I love you.

CHAPTER 127

ELAINE COULDN'T WAIT to see Charlie and called the moment she arrived home.

"Hello," Charlie said.

"I want you," Elaine said immediately.

"Who is this?" Charlie asked teasingly, knowing exactly who it was.

"This is your special lover. Let's meet, and I'll show you who I really am. I'll show you all of me. I'll show you every part of me. You can look, feel, touch, hold, lick, and take in my essence and do anything you want to me. Then you will for sure know who I am." Elaine seductively sighed and moaned into the phone.

"OK, meet me at the Tradewinds Motel in an hour."

Charlie heard the receiver go to a dial tone and knew he'd better hurry, calling to mind a few new things he had learned at Grace Bar and Grill.

CHAPTER 128

REGINA WALKED TO the dining room, where her morning coffee and biscotti were waiting, along with the morning newspaper. She glanced at the front page: "THE WAR IN EUROPE IS ENDED! SURRENDER IS UNCONDITIONAL; V E WILL BE PROCLAIMED TODAY!"

Regina made the sign of the cross, finishing with a kiss to her hand.

"Thank God. And thank you, God, for what this family has escaped by your will. Michael, Michael, look! Come read with me."

"What are you making this racket about?" he asked, walking in to join her, tying his tie at the same time.

"Look, the war is finally over. Look, look! And way down here, it says, Allied forces closed in on Milan, and Italian dictator Benito Mussolini was captured by Italian partisans as he was trying to escape to Switzerland and was executed in Giulino. His body was taken to Milan and hung up for the public to see."

"*Che vergogna!* A disgrace!" Michael said. "We need to contact Adonis and Mechelina to see how bad the vineyard has become and if we need to send money to help them get the wine crates they buried dug up and out of the hills to restart shipping back here. Our inventory has dropped a lot according to Frank and Maria."

"Michael, we will do that today. Charlie is asking if there are any apartments available for Elaine. She wants to be out on her own now that she has a position with Pell Global Group."

"You know more about what is available. If you have to, check with Horace. . Just take care of it and be sure it's in one of the better buildings we have in Manhattan."

"Oh, I know. I love the Sutton Tower building on Sutton Place South. You know the one, right on the river near Fifty-Seventh Street. I'll have Theresa see what's available there. How is Adele doing?"

"They just got back from that hospital in the Midwest that treats people when other doctors can't find out what's wrong with them," Michael said. "Izzy will be back in the office today. What are you doing today?"

"I'm going to work on this apartment for Elaine. I have some meetings with Theresa and Gina to finalize Bobby and Patty's place. And I have to find out if we can get Nick's Arrow back out on the track circuit. I'll meet up with you later."

"Adonis and Mechelina," Michael said. "That's the first thing." He walked out, carrying his coffee cup with him.

CHAPTER 129

FRANK AND MARIA began to prepare the warehouse and the workers for the influx of the hundreds of cases that would contain Terreno Rico wines, imported from the Adonis Winery, which would then be shipped to the distribution centers Charlie had devised and set up.

Frank was constantly thinking of ways to make more sales and place more wine

"I've come up with an idea for the salesmen to push the wine," he told Maria. "We need them to push cases and not bottles, right? For every six cases they place in one location, they will get fifteen dollars off. They need to be told."

"You're brilliant. We can get this information out to everyone in plenty of time. Regina said that the wine should be arriving in a month or so. I have to meet Regina and Theresa. I'll see you later."

CHAPTER 130

CONCERNED FOR ADELE and her well-being, Michael, Vince, and Bill met with Izzy to offer whatever it was they could help with.

"Regina has been visiting with Adele, which is a help," Izzy said. "I can't believe what the doctors found."

"What's going on? Tell us," Bill said, remembering how difficult it was when his wife, Mary, became ill and died.

"They found she has this rare fucking thing called porphyria," Izzy said with disdain. "It causes skin problems, abdominal pain, cramps, vomiting, mental disorders, and seizures."

"What the fuck causes this?" asked Vince.

"Some fucking thing in her blood doesn't work right. There's no cure. She's supposed to stay away from cigarettes, alcohol, sun, sedatives, and every fucking thing she does and likes. It can become serious, and she can become paranoid, which I've seen her do. The doctors say blood transfusions may help to reduce what's in her blood. She ain't gonna stay away from all the shit she likes."

"Izzy, do whatever you need to do and take her anywhere that can help," Michael said. "Don't worry about what it costs. You're family to me."

"Thank you. Let me tell you about the Colony Hotel. I've got to get my mind off this sick shit. I'll have to leave soon. This is a great fucking hotel. It has it all with one exception: entertainment! This place is gorgeous. We could add space right onto the existing building for shows. We can bring in top names. It's known as the Pink Jewel of Miami. The staff, the grounds, the food are all top-notch. Hollywood stars go there for a stay because it's so quiet. This place could turn into a real moneymaker for us. It's too quiet; it has to be jazzed up."

"Good job," Bill said.

"Go ahead, Izzy. We've got you covered here," Vince said.

"Thanks, Izzy," Michael said. "Let me know what you or Adele need. I'll call Conrad. I guess he's looking for a piece of this place if we can take it off their hands for a decent price. He has some money in his pocket that we can use. He wants us to run it and build it."

"Only thing, who are we going to put there?" Michael asked. "I'm confident that we are going to snag this gem. The owner is a big gambler and owes a shitload of cash. Conrad said he's willing to deal and wants to keep a piece of the place. That's not going to fit in our plans. Who can we use to get rid of this pest?"

"Not to worry," Izzy said. "It'll be a piece of cake. I'll take care of it myself. We don't have to bring anyone in. As soon as it's ours and I get Adele stable, I'll visit and take care of the pest. Charlotte said she'll stay with Adele anytime."

CHAPTER 131

JIMMY COHEN, BOBBY Valentine's manager, was ecstatic when he spoke to Michael over the telephone, from California. "This has been an amazing ride, thanks to you and your group, Michael. We want to invite everyone out for the premiere of Bobby's new movie, *Shadow*. He plays a gumshoe, and the studio is so happy, they are considering a few follow-up movies. I, *we*, can't thank you enough. The premiere is in three weeks. I can have my office make all the arrangements for you and your group. We're looking forward to everyone coming."

"Well, thanks, Jimmy. We accept. I'll get everyone on board and let you know what's going on with it. It's a good gesture on your part. I look forward to seeing the blue sky and the sunshine."

"OK, then I'll get things rolling. Talk soon."

Michael thought for a moment. *Hmm, there's our opening act for the Colony Hotel.*

CHAPTER 132

CHARLIE WALKED INTO Elaine's office with flowers.

"Oh, Charlie, these are beautiful," Elaine said happily. "Thank you."

"Not as beautiful as you," he said.

"Come here." Elaine wrapped her arms around him, kissing him passionately. "What do you say, Charlie?" she asked provocatively.

"Here? Are you nuts?" he asked shyly.

"Come on, I want to show you where you're going to live." Elaine grabbed Charlie's hand and her coat. "You know your parents got me into Sutton Tower just around the corner. You're going to love it!"

It was only a brisk walk from her office to the front entrance, which housed a doorman in full regalia, with gold braids attached to huge tassels. His cap looked like a general's. He opened the door with a greeting.

"Good morning, Miss Solofra. Charlie, I haven't seen you for quite a while."

"Thank you, good morning," Elaine said.

"Wow, Leo, it has been a while. I hope your family is doing well. You'll be seeing quite a bit of me," Charlie told Leo. They passed into a lobby that was like a hotel's, filled with mirrors, marble, velvet couches, and chairs.

"Don't you want to come home to this at night, Charlie?" Elaine asked, planting a thought but not expecting an answer. "You already know Leo."

The elevator ride was as smooth as the kisses they were giving each other until the elevator came to a stop with a slight bounce. Elaine slid the brass scissor-gate door open, leading Charlie to her apartment. She opened the door to picture-perfect décor and a fantastic view of the East River.

"Wow! I knew Mother and Gina were busy decorating this for you, but I had no idea," Charlie said. "This is magnificent. Pell Group treats its people with class. I love it, Elaine. It fits you perfectly."

"It fits you too, you know."

Elaine proceeded to the kitchen to make some coffee, Charlie right behind.

After filling the pot with water, she counted the scoops to put in the pot, turning to look at Charlie with an impish smile. Elaine removed her blouse and stepped out of her skirt, standing there in her little bra and panties.

I am in awe of her beauty, as usual, Charlie thought.

In what seemed like slow motion, Elaine reached behind her back and unhooked her bra, tossing it to join the rest of her clothes.

Standing there almost naked, Charlie became transfixed on her perfectly shaped breasts with areolas that resembled milk chocolate. He watched her nipples stand at attention with his gaze.

"I know you like these," Elaine said, grabbing her breasts from the bottom, pushing them up.

"I love them."

Elaine slowly untied Charlie's tie and unbuttoned his shirt as he loosened his belt. Her hand moved to lower his trousers' zipper as Charlie kicked off his shoes.

"You're"—he took a deep breath—"magnificent."

He placed his hand into her panties and stroked his fingers up and down her pussy, which was now moist.

Charlie helped Elaine take off the rest his clothes, staring in adoration at this Venus. No matter how many times he saw Elaine nude, it was a magical moment for him.

Elaine took hold of Charlie's manhood as he sighed deeply.

Leaning in toward each other, their lips touched, caressing with little love bites. Elaine's soft toilet water fragrance ignited his senses, helping his cock grow harder. She squeezed it tighter with one hand and gently rubbed his balls with the other.

Elaine, taking charge, guided Charlie to the couch, laying them both down and pushing Charlie's head toward her throbbing cunt. He absorbed her beautiful scent. Her lovely lips were soaking wet as Charlie licked all around, gently sucking her clit. Elaine moaned as she continued to gyrate her hips. Just as Charlie was getting into a comfortable position, Elaine pulled him up toward her, kissing him as she grabbed his pulsating cock and inserted it in her soaking-wet, waiting vagina.

"Do you like that?" Elaine asked.

Charlie took a moment of silence to enjoy her warmth and wetness.

"I don't like it," he finally answered. Feeling her tense in response to his words, he quickly added, "I love it, and I love you. You're with me every moment."

Elaine's soft, choked moans in Charlie's ear were enthralling as she thrust with his rhythms, digging her nails into his ass to guide him as he pumped into her crying cunt.

"Ah! Yes! I just came. Oahu! Go, go. Finish inside me." Elaine directed; she wanted control.

Charlie did as commanded, holding her and kissing softly as he withdrew. Lying there naked, Elaine stroked her hand through Charlie's hair.

"You know I have to go to California for the premiere of Bobby Valentine's new movie," she said. "When I'm gone, why don't you move your things in here with me?"

"You know, I just might do that," Charlie said. "My parents will be going too. It might be a good time. I'll let them know before they leave, so my mother won't be in shock. I know my old man won't mind."

CHAPTER 133

WHILE THE CAT'S away, the mice will play, and so they did. Most of the key people from Pell Global Group were in California for the movie premiere. With Izzy dealing with Adele's sudden illness and Elaine in California, both Izzy and Charlie made a trip to visit Anna Charme at Grace Bar and Grill. This time, Charlie had the envelope for Anna and planned to do some shopping both for information and for additional ways to please Elaine.

Izzy explained the problems with the disease Adele was dealing with. "At times, it's worse than others, Charlie. There is no cure, and the doctors are trying to treat this fucking thing. It's in her blood. It makes her skin itch, swell, and sometimes blister. Worse of all, she becomes unmanageable sometimes with depression, and then she hallucinates that she is facing soldiers, lined up."

"I'm sorry, Izzy," Charlie said. "You must be feeling that this is fucked up, and it is when there's nothing you can do about it."

"Yeah, I know. You know your father and me have been together forever. And now, watching you grow—one day, Charlie, it will all be yours."

"I understand, Izzy. Everyone who is with us will always be with us. We are family. You, Vince, and Bill are like my uncles. Is there anything else we can do for Adele?"

"No, Charlie thanks. I'm going to park around back."

"Ah!" said Anna, with a big hug and kiss for Charlie. With Izzy, she held on to him, whispering in his ear, "I'm so sorry to hear about Adele. I miss her. I hope things turn out well for you both. She's a good girl, Izzy. Stay with her." Stepping away, she added, "Is today business or pleasure?"

Charlie handed Anna the envelope. Anna smiled and said, "Oh, I see, both today. Let me call the girls, and we'll talk later. I have news for you both."

CHAPTER 134

"REGINA, CALM DOWN and lower your voice," Michael commanded Regina, his own voice raised. "Charlie and Elaine are adults. We don't live in the Old Country. As a matter of fact, you were born in America, and we were fucking long before we were married, remember? This is the nineteen forties, and it's a new generation. Times change. Look how we made changes, even our name."

"All right, all right," Regina stammered, sounding curt as the edge of her lip curled. "I see what you're saying and what you're getting at. We didn't just fuck; we made love then and still do," Regina said arrogantly.

"Yeah, we did, and we still do...make love. It was great then and it is great now. We don't know, but I imagine they feel the same for each other as we did and do now. Don't you think so?"

"I hope so. I love Elaine. She is good for Charlie. I just..."

"You just what? Want them to be like us? Be happy and successful and maybe have children? Well, me too. I want nothing but good for both of them."

"Come here," Regina said, changing her demeanor. She held her arms open and then held Michael tightly.

"You know, everyone is out of the house, even the staff and Miss Rosa," Regina said, opening her silk robe and letting it drop to the floor, exposing her natural self.

"You see," Michael whispered as Regina unbuttoned his pajamas. "Don't you think they...?" Regina held her finger to his mouth to be quiet. She knew where he was going but certainly did not want to hear it. She continued to pull Michael's pajama bottoms down, bending herself to the level of his pants. She took his already-erect cock in her hand and guided it into her mouth.

CHAPTER 135

THE WAR MANPOWER Commission was established via Presidential Executive Order number 9139. The function of the WMC was to determine the need for employment in various industries. The WMC coordinated with labor unions on programs such as the Employment Stabilization Plan, which aimed to place workers in specific jobs during the war. Bill Sullivan, being the labor leader, represented labor in meetings held by WMC to discuss labor and management issues. Bill was a huge influence in getting the WMC to understand the importance of the return of thoroughbred horse racing after the war ended.

In his statement to the WMC, he said, "This is an opportunity to raise the spirit of Americans to realize we are going to be bigger and better as a nation. The return to the sport of kings will help America grow. It will bring revenue to the government and the people. It is going to raise another opportunity for growth and employment, making individuals feel good about themselves. You will not be disappointed!"

Bill Sullivan was right. Revenues from the horse-racing industry soon totaled over four hundred million dollars for the year.

Bill gave Elaine the assignment of getting Nick's Arrow back on the racing circuit and handling all the legal bullshit that went with it, including contracts for Billy Jackson and Eddie Hudson. Regina agreed to having Elaine take this assignment over since Regina was too busy overseeing financial records.

CHAPTER 136

ELAINE AND CHARLIE sat in the living room, looking out at a beautiful skyline of the East River, the lights glimmering. Both were sipping wine.

"I am so grateful for the position with Pell Global Group," Elaine said. "I'm handling Nick's Arrow, Bobby Valentine's issues and his contracts, and now Regina has me looking at the real estate holdings. I love you and your family, Charlie. I have to go to Miami with Horace for the closing deal on the Colony Hotel. I put in the contract that three suites will always be available. One for the entertainers who will be appearing there and two for whoever Pell Group wants to comp, even us."

"Sounds brilliant, Elaine. Three suites empty all year out of one hundred fifty rooms won't put a damper on the revenue, particularly since we are going to be adding entertainment. The liquor sales alone will more than make up for it, let alone the cost for the shows. I heard it's a gem of a place, according to Izzy and Adele. It's known as the Pink Jewel of Miami Beach."

"Want to come with me?" Elaine asked, reaching for Charlie's hand.

"I have to pass. I'm working with Izzy, gathering information on the gambling degenerate Morris Hoffman, who we're buying the hotel from. I'm real close to getting what I'll need."

"What kind of information do we need?"

"You know my father had you and Horace put in the contract that Morris will maintain a ten percent holding? That was going to be the only way we were able to go ahead with this deal."

"I was questioning your father on that. He insisted, so I had to put it in."

"The money Morris is getting from the sale is supposed to pay the people he owes money to for his gambling. We know he's not going to stop gambling. We can't have these people hanging around when he goes in debt to them again. It will be bad for business. These guys will soon know who the new owners are and how we do business. One thing I learned in school is math doesn't lie. One and one always equals two. So, the ten percent is going to be short-lived, *capire?* We will send a loud and clear message announcing the new owners."

"Oh! I understand. I'd like to be there when that goes down," Elaine said, reaching over to kiss Charlie. "C'mon." She stood up in front of the huge windows, undressing and throwing her clothes onto the sofa. "For now, I'll be the one going down." They worked their way into the bedroom.

CHAPTER 137

THE SALE OF the Colony Hotel to Pell Global Group went as smoothly as putting cream in your coffee. The ink wasn't even dry when construction started to add an extension that would be a nightclub, dining room, and bar, where the high-powered entertainers would be performing.

No time was wasted with the information about Morris Hoffman that Anna Charme had given to Charlie and Izzy on their last visit. Both the Hoffmans were in their late sixties and in failing health, which was one of the reasons Morris was in such debt. He had been trying to pay all the medical bills, thinking he could hedge himself with heavy gambling. Anna was able to give the Hoffmans' schedule to Charlie and Izzy down to the minute of each day.

Morris was upset with giving up his ownership and that both he and his wife had failing health. He would drink himself into a stupor most days before driving home for an afternoon nap, returning to the hotel later in the evening.

Izzy was staying at a nearby motel under a different name when he received the call he was waiting for. He checked out of the motel and drove the route to the Hoffmans' house. He followed the instructions he had to the letter:

Head south on Orange Ridge Road to the Collins Bridge, crossing over.

Head west to Avenue D.

Head south to Miami Avenue, to a neighborhood called Florida City.

There is an archway on your right when you enter into a neighborhood with upper-class two-story homes.

Turn left on Brickell Ave to number 114.

Enter through sliding door at back of house, always unlocked for easy access to the swimming pool.

Right on the button, Izzy thought, slipping on a pair of gloves and checking the .22-caliber revolver he was going to use. The .22 was called an assassin's choice because the bullet enters, rattles around, and does not exit. You had to be up close and personal to get a quality hit.

Izzy quietly slid the glass door open just enough to fit through with minimal noise. Looking through doorway, he saw Mrs. Hoffman sitting in the kitchen, reading the racing form for the horses running at the Miami Jockey Club. She sipped her tea as she made notes next to what horses she wanted to place bets on.

That Anna is amazing with the information she is able to get, thought Izzy. *The old lady is exactly where the details said she would be.*

Without hesitation, Izzy stepped behind her, putting the small-caliber pistol to the back of her head and firing once. He watched her body slump forward. She looked like she had fallen asleep with her head on the table, with one exception: blood was pouring out her head and down her face, dripping drop by drop onto the floor. Quickly going up the stairs to the second level, Izzy saw Morris sitting on the bed, his feet on the floor and the rest of his body lying back, passed out.

Izzy lifted Morris up to a sitting position, remembering the devil is in the details. He called to mind the instructions that read "M.H—left-handed."

"Goddamn it!" Izzy said out loud. He laid Morris back down just as he was starting to mumble in a drunken stupor. Izzy went to his left side to again lift him to a sitting position, putting the revolver in Morris's left hand and pointing it to his left temple. Izzy pulled the trigger.

Done, he thought. The newspapers would read, "Hotel magnate kills wife, commits suicide."

CHAPTER 138

SIX MONTHS HAD passed since construction started on the addition to the Colony Hotel.

The grand opening for the Supper Club finally arrived, with headliner Bobby Valentine. The Pells had everyone from Pell Global Group staying at the hotel for a week, including a few distinguished guests such as Senator Silver, Miami Mayor Henry Delson (handpicked by the Pell Group), actors and actresses from Bobby's movie *Shadow*, and top names from the silver screen: Greta Marr; the two blond bombshell Webb sisters, Diana and Emily; and leading man Jonathan Donavan; along with music director and arranger, Marshall Stein. The list was an enormous who's who.

Photographers and reporters were clamoring to get in. Flashbulbs popped as they all tried to get a photo, and maybe a few words, of the movie stars and dignitaries. This event was first class all the way, in the Pell fashion. Men wore tuxedos, with women in designer dresses. There was a red carpet with some sort of glitter on it. The photographers were calling out to the Hollywood people, hoping the stars would turn for a better picture.

"Greta, over here! Look here."

"Diana, can you and Johnathan hold hands? Emily, now you, hold Johnathan's arm."

Limousines were pulling up one after the other. All of a sudden, a white carriage with two well-groomed white horses pulled up. The roar of the crowd was deafening when the groomsman opened the door and Bobby Valentine stepped out dressed in white, from head to toe. He was followed by his wife, Patty, also in white.

Bobby and Patty were stunning standing on the red, glittering carpet as they posed for pictures, shook hands, and signed autographs. This event had been the creative genius of Theresa and Gina Ponti.

"Brilliant" was the word used over and over in the newspaper's social column the next day.

"Bobby's performance was brilliant. After changing into a black tuxedo and walking out to a packed house, Bobby opened with his signature song, 'As Time Goes By,' taking the audience into another time and place.

"The new décor will be known for its brilliance.

"The brilliancy of the diamond-shaped stage will be a feature for future acts.

"Every aspect of this grand opening performance was just brilliant, brilliant, brilliant."

CHAPTER 139

TIME WAS APPROACHING to start to groom Samuel Roberts for the presidential campaign. Sam and his wife, Priscilla, were willing to take on the grueling schedule necessary to bring them into the public eye.

Michael explained his reasoning for choosing Ronald Silver for the inner circle as soon as those serving coffee left the meeting room.

"Ron is the first governor to win an election in his first primary and defeat five other candidates. His state of Florida has little disorder compared to other states because he upheld capital punishment. He initiated his own radio program to discuss the concerns of the people in his state. He chaired the Democratic National Convention. Remember how he helped the United States with its dealing in Cuba? He is well-known, respected, and loved by people throughout the country. Having Ron in the number-two position will just give him time to ripen for the number-one position in eight years when Sam's term ends. Anyone have questions?"

"I have a slogan for the campaign," Elaine said.

"Well, let's hear it, Elaine," Regina called out.

"All right. What do you all think? 'Sam is the man with a voice that won't echo.'"

Eyebrows raised, heads nodding up and down in agreement. Smiles broadened as Michael looked at each person, going around the table.

"Good thinking, Elaine," Michael said. "So, anything Sam says will never bounce back in his face, and he won't be labeled a hypocrite. Let's go with it."

Within the Pell Group, everyone and everything moved smoothly, quickly, and on time—completely on the other side of the spectrum compared to

Washington. They knew once Sam got into office, they would have a strong influence on his decisions.

"Theresa, you will be in charge of all the travel arrangements, hotels, buses, and whatever is needed," Michael said. "Of course, Elaine and Horace will be our legal advisors. Regina, use the best artist you can find to help do the designs. , and we'll reconvene in one month on this. Bill, see how any unions have to play into this. We're done, everybody. Go."

The room emptied. As Michael walked to his office, he was thinking of the next step. "One step ahead of the shoeshine," he remembered telling his customers as a kid.

The Pell Global Group inner circle continued to widen as individuals were added to help the wheel turn as smoothly as possible. The right amount of cogs turns the wheel just at the right speed, especially when they are those you can trust.

"Detective, I understand you are ready to retire," Michael said to John the Pipe.

"Yes, Mr. Pell. I was thinking of getting my pension and buying a cab or limousine. I have about three to four months before I pull the trigger, so to speak." He laughed heartily at his own humor.

"Well, John, would you be interested in doing private bodyguard work full-time for us, a certain detail that will take you around the country?"

"I'd be very interested, Mr. Pell. What would it entail?"

"For now, I can tell you it will be protection for a presidential candidate. The Secret Service will carry the brunt of it, but we need our own people involved. I would like you to get a few more of you, say two more. You will lead our group. Your pay will be double your salary as a detective. Remember, we need men we can trust with our lives, like you, John."

"You can rely on me, Mr. Pell. I'll get a group together. I am really looking forward to this assignment."

CHAPTER 140

SOME OF THE Pell Group arrived at the New York State Executive Mansion, the official residence of Governor Roberts and his wife, Priscilla, along with Lieutenant Governor Cunningham and his wife, Lilly.

Regina, Theresa, Gina Ponti, Izzy, Bill Sullivan, and their detective detail were met by Priscilla and Lilly.

After short introductions, Priscilla announced, "While lunch is being prepared, let us take you on a brief tour."

Lilly went on to say, "Follow me if you will." She led everyone down the hall, pointing to different pictures and rooms.

"Before this magnificent Italianate building was restored to its present beauty, it was owned by a prominent business industrialist and was destroyed in a fire. Rather than having it restored, he donated the property to the historical society, giving the restoration its beauty along with the stale, musty odor"—this brought a smile to everyone's face—"thus the home we are now standing in. Over the years, the different governors and their wives have added on to their liking, such as the tennis court and the steam room."

"I understand, Ms. Ponti, you are a very successful decorator who is in much demand," Priscilla added. "I would love to have your services down the road." She gave a wink as she glanced toward Izzy.

"On the second level," Lilly continued, "you will see our living space." Priscilla moved ahead of everyone. When she reached an open door, she closed it, slowly turning to the group but directly looking at Izzy.

"This is my private room," Priscilla said in a pleasant tone. "There's nothing special in here, folks. It's a mess. I'll just close the door. Lilly keeps her room much tidier."

Each of the others looked at one another with a quizzical crunch of their eyebrows. Just then, there was a loud ring of a bell.

"It's time for lunch," Lilly said, pointing to guide the visitors toward the dining room. "Watch your step on the stairs."

Priscilla stepped between Bill and Izzy so she could put her arms in each of theirs to guide them to the stairs.

CHAPTER 141

LUNCH BROUGHT ON the small talk of where everyone was from, how everyone grew up, and the struggles each of them overcame to reach their present positions.

Soon the table was cleared, and Lilly suggested they move into the conference room to discuss the campaign colors, slogan, and travel arrangements. Detective John was invited to have coffee with the state troopers who were always in the house. Priscilla took Izzy by the arm.

"All this campaign stuff is best left to Lilly," she said. "Sam and Bert agree. I have very little interest and patience for the party planning and why unions have to build the stage and all of that. I just like to show up for the party. I'll show Mr. Soloman the garden." As they strolled out the French doors to the garden, they could hear the chatter of the others.

Izzy slowed his step to keep pace with Priscilla. "Thank you for saving me from all that."

"You mean all that bullshit," she said.

"Yeah, I guess you can call it that."

"You know, Izzy...I can call you Izzy?"

"Of course you can."

"You can call me Priscilla. I'm sorry to hear about your wife being so sick and all. Adele and I were in the same business. I was called Prissy. We never knew each other, and no one knows it. It was a long time ago for me and in another country."

"How did you know about Adele, and why are you telling me?" Izzy asked.

"Information is crucial, particularly in politics, don't you agree? Turn here." She opened a set of doors leading to a back hallway.

After climbing a staircase, Priscilla guided them to another door. She reached into her bra to pull out a skeleton key. When she opened her private room, she gave Izzy the sign to keep quiet.

"Let me close the connecting door to Lilly's room." She quietly turned the knob, careful not to make a sound.

"Interesting you have adjoining rooms," Izzy said, almost posing it as a question.

"I told you, I was in the same business as Adele. Lilly and I keep each other...shall I say, entertained."

Izzy's mind was racing with thoughts of Priscilla and Lilly together. Soon he was fully aroused.

"Come here and take my clothes off," Priscilla said. "No kissing. Just fuck me. Fuck me hard."

CHAPTER 142

"JESUS CHRIST! IZZY! What the fuck did you do, banging the governor's wife? I know she is quite a lady, but, Izzy, really!" Michael angrily demanded an answer.

"Michael, Michael, calm down." Izzy was practically shouting. "Priscilla took me by the hand while everyone else was discussing the campaign material to show me the garden. We wound up in her private room, and she demanded that I take her clothes off and fuck her. She told me that she was a prostitute in Canada many years ago when she was in her early twenties and she knew Adele was in the same business. She was called Prissy, and she and Lilly sometimes entertain each other. They each have their own private connected rooms aside from their marriage bedrooms."

Seeing Michael had calmed down, Izzy went on. "None of this came out when we got Sam the governor's office. You know who can also stop information from passing hands? Anna, Grace Bar and Grill. You and I can pay her a visit to be sure she can't divulge any of this."

"Maybe we should. I still can't figure out why Priscilla told you about herself. I don't blame you for fucking her. She is—"

At that moment the door opened, with Regina, Theresa, and Gina Ponti standing there. "I'm sorry," Regina said. "We didn't know the conference room was in use. We can come back.

"No, no," said Izzy. "We're finished."

"Take Charlie with you," Michael said to Izzy on the way out.

Regina glanced at her husband without any expression. She knew never to ask about certain matters, but she'd never forgotten the burning question always in her mind: Who shot whom on Charlie's seventh birthday some twenty years ago?

CHAPTER 143

"Izzy, Charlie, you never need an invite or appointment," Anna Charme said with delight. "Come, let's go to the lounge."

"We need to speak with you, Anna," Charlie said.

"Uh-oh! Sounds serious. Come with me to my office." Anna led the way.

"There is some information about Priscilla Roberts that we found out, and she knew about Adele and her past," Izzy said.

"Priscilla Roberts, the governor's wife?" Anna asked. "I don't know anything about her or where she gets her information. Remember, politics makes strange bedfellows. Shakespeare, you know. We're not the only ones in the information business, Izzy. I know where my bread is buttered and believe me, I would never spill any information from the Pells or their associates. Do you think I want another Thirty-Fourth Street Barbershop incident here? If anything should come my way, you both know and so does Michael, I would contact you immediately. Is there anything in particular you need to tell me so I can dig further for you both? I'm in your bed only."

"No, Anna," Charlie said. "Not at the moment."

"Well then, c'mon. Let me line up the ladies for you both. This one is on the house. I'll take care of the girls."

CHAPTER 144

ELAINE CALLED OUT to Charlie as she poured coffee in their cups. "Do you want bacon and eggs or pancakes? I'm pouring coffee, so c'mon. Get up. Let's do something. It's Sunday."

Charlie came up behind her, giving her a kiss on the neck, but Elaine flinched.

"Shit, Charlie, you scared me. Wow, you've showered already. You smell good. Hey, you're kind of sexy in your towel. Here's your coffee. What do you want for breakfast?"

"Mmm, just one slice of toast and an egg. Nothing fancy, thanks. Do you have something in mind for today?"

"As a matter of fact, I do," said Elaine. "Let's take a ride to Yonkers. Nick's Arrow is training and running some laps. I think we should show our faces and not leave it all to Billy Jackson. I spoke to Regina, and she said if we go, they would meet us there and would enjoy a day without bodyguards and photographers. They don't have anything on their agenda either. It will be good for us to be seen by as many horse people as possible, as often as possible."

"OK. You know, Elaine, I found out something about that infamous shooting at the Thirty-Fourth Street Barbershop—"

"Oh yeah, I remember hearing about it over the years. That was a long time ago."

"Yes, it was my father's doing when he was involved with Cuba's Hotel En El Mar's gambling and prostitution."

"Are you fucking kidding me? Wow, c'mon. We have time. I haven't showered yet. Don't be kidding me around. Just fuck me." She pulled off the towel

Charlie had on from the shower, throwing it on the floor. "Do you think I'd make a good prostitute?"

"You'd be my favorite, like Izzy and Adele were to each other," Charlie said.

"OK, I'm your whore. Tell me what you want me to do for you!" Elaine grabbed his hands and rushed to the bed.

CHAPTER 145

THE DAY AT Central City Racetrack was a clear, beautiful day with a chill that required a light jacket or sweater. Regina, Michael, Charlie, and Elaine leaned on the rail fence, each using a pair of binoculars to watch Nick's Arrow gallop the track as jockey Eddie Hudson kept breaking his own record.

It was nice to have lunch with Conrad and Doris in a quiet setting, not having all the hangers-on creating chaos in Conrad's private dining room. As usual, Conrad had his favorite lunch served.

Conrad raised his wineglass, saying, "A toast," waiting for everyone to raise their glasses. "May we have much success with Nick's Arrow in the coming years." Everyone's raised wineglass touched the others, and the *tinging* represented the "amen" at the end of a prayer.

"Tell me how things are going with the presidential campaign," Conrad said.

"Great, Conrad," Regina said. "We have a campaign slogan, and arrangements are being made for traveling, hotels, cities with stopovers, storefront rentals for each town's campaign headquarters. So we've gotten a lot accomplished already."

"Don't keep us in suspense, dear," Doris said. "What is the campaign slogan?"

"Go ahead, Elaine, you thought of it. You claim it. Tell it to the Millers. It's brilliant, Doris."

"All right: 'Sam is the man with a voice that won't echo.'"

"Very good, dear," Doris said.

"Good? I love it!" Conrad said. "It's perfect. What Sam said on the campaign trail or in his speeches won't come back to haunt him in the future. You're a bright young lady, Elaine. Charlie, you are one lucky son of a bitch!"

"Yes, Conrad, I am. I love her," Charlie claimed just as Elaine reached for Charlie's hand resting on the table. Regina tilted her head with a smile on her face, holding back her tears.

"You two must be very proud of their accomplishments," Doris said, looking at Michael and Regina.

"We certainly are," Regina said. "We love them both and are so happy Elaine is part of our family and our business. She has been an outstanding asset who has accomplished many good things for us all. We'll keep her."

Everyone chuckled in response.

Conrad quickly raised his wineglass for another toast.

"To Charlie and Elaine. Good luck and good love."

CHAPTER 146

THE INNER CIRCLE'S regular meetings for updates and reports on all activities had proven productive.

"Who's up first?" Charlie asked.

"I've got great reports from Frank and Maria," Vince said. "The wine outlets are doing much better since Frank started that bonus program for the salesmen. The figures are up by twenty-five percent from last year already, with new accounts opening each week."

"I've recently heard from Italy...cousins Adonis, Mechelina, and Benevento," Charlie said. "They are so thankful for our distribution; they had to add on more buildings and people. They are the town's heroes. They can't wait to see us. Whoever came up with the idea to move the wine to Switzerland saved both us and them."

Elaine put in her two cents. "Horace needs to check with all the new accounts that their liquor license is up-to-date with the state liquor authority. I'll be sure to review this with him."

"I spoke with Regina this morning," Bill said. "She is working hard on the campaign, with her group accomplishing a lot. Some towns I've contacted don't require a union to do the stage building, so we're ahead of the game there. The places that do, I have under control. No worries."

Charlie gave Elaine a look as a signal that she should leave the room, and she did, excusing herself. Just like Regina, she had learned her place in the pecking order of the Pell family and the Pell Global Group.

"OK, anything we need to discuss with information from Charme?" Michael asked.

Everyone shook their heads no.

"I want to thank everyone for helping me deal with Adele," Izzy said. "You know I've basically had to hire Charlotte as a full-time companion for her. She's been going to Bellevue Hospital Center for observation and to change her medication a lot. We haven't even had sex in months, probably closer to a year. She seems to be getting worse."

"We know it's not been easy for you, Izzy," Michael said. "That Bellevue Hospital is good. My mother went there for her tuberculosis, but it was too late for her. It's not too late for Adele. Why don't you frequent Anna Charme and her girls? It will be good for you. You need an outlet, unless you want another assignment like the Hoffmans."

Everyone laughed. "Right now, I think I'll visit Adele and Charlotte at the hospital," Izzy said. "However, you never know."

"Izzy," Michael called out, "stop paying Charlotte. Pell Group will pay her with a raise. I'll tell Theresa to set it up. Now go!"

CHAPTER 147

MICHAEL OPENED THE door to their new Cadillac Series 6200 Convertible, as he always did for Regina.

The interior was pure luxury, with the most supple burgundy leather and the reflective Madeira Maroon Poly exterior paint accented with a tan color cloth top, along with a low, sleek, torpedo-style body that housed a slant on the windshield and a curved rear window. This Cadillac looked and drove like a dream.

Whenever Michael received compliments about the car, he would always say, "Regina, you turn more heads from both men and women than this new Caddy, whether the top is up or down."

The door closed, and Michael got into the driver's seat to start the engine. He drove out of the parking area of the Central City Rack Track.

"That was a nice surprise to finally see Nick's Arrow win a race," Regina said with a charming lilt to her voice.

"Yes, and Conrad with his special dinners and toasts always makes you smile."

Regina just could not hold back any longer.

"I have to ask you, Michael," she said, quivering not with fear but out of anger. "Many, many years ago, I heard Vince and Izzy talking in the hallway on my way out of a meeting with Horace. It's plagued me all these years. You have no idea how many sleepless nights I've endured or how much I've paced the floor, always having this plaguing me, never able to share it with anyone. They were talking about someone who was murdered on Charlie's seventh birthday. I need to know, and I need to know now! Were they speaking about you? Did you kill someone?"

Michael turned on the windshield wipers as it started to drizzle. He glared out at the darkness, and the traffic light turned green for him to go. As he pulled onto Central City Boulevard to turn left and head south to their Riverdale mansion, he turned to see Regina staring at him, waiting for his answer. At the same time, he saw headlights from another car speeding toward them, running the red traffic light. Not stopping, the car plowed forward charging like an armored tank racing to the front lines. "Regina, I love you," Michael said nervously. These were the last words Michael and Regina ever spoke or heard.

The speeding car hit them square on, crushing the side of the car where Regina was sitting and pushing their Cadillac into the service road wall. The other car continued to roll onto the convertible top, crushing both Michael and Regina and killing them instantly.

The detail of detectives following in a separate car looked on at the horrific sight.

Both cars were mangled into crushed steel and glass in only a matter of seconds. People ran out from the corner bar upon hearing the crash, and then started to scream as the horn from the Cadillac continued to blare. Detective John jumped from his car before it had come to a complete stop, yelling for someone to get a bucket of water to throw on the gasoline he could smell.

Detective John rushed to the Cadillac, where he saw both Michael and Regina buried and crushed. There was blood everywhere and internal organs splattered. Glancing over at Regina, he became nauseated.

"Oh my God, she's been decapitated!" Yelling in a shocked voice, he said, "Where's her fucking head?" He kept shouting out, "Where's her fucking head? Goddamn it, find her head!" He had never witnessed anything like it in twenty years as a policeman.

After telling the spectators to go back in the bar, and call the police and an ambulance, someone ran with water in a bucket.

"Quick, throw it here," John shouted. "Get more, and hurry up." The expressions on the bar patrons' faces were confusion, shock, and fear. They were almost in a frozen state, barely able to move.

The police, fire trucks, and ambulance were there in minutes, spraying some sort of fire-retardant foam to prevent an explosion. Emergency vehicles arrived on the scene one after the other, with their sirens blasting and lights flashing.

All of the bar patrons were clamoring as they gathered in the rain to watch. The lights from the police cars, fire trucks, and ambulance added to the hectic, abnormal, confusing scene.

Someone pointed up toward the car sitting on top of the Cadillac.

"Oh my God, look!" he shouted. "Someone is moving in that car up there."

A fireman climbed to the top car as soon as a ladder was in place to see that the driver was just dazed and regaining consciousness.

"Jesus Christ, it's a priest, and he is drunk as a skunk!" the fireman yelled back down.

Detective John flashed his badge to one of the patrolmen and said, "Arrest that son of a bitch, now!" He approached the police sergeant now in charge of the scene and identified himself and the occupants of the Cadillac. Immediately, the sergeant ordered two of the cops to get statements from the bar patrons about the driver's condition in the bar.

"Holy shit, no fucking way. The famous Pell family?" the sergeant asked John. "This is going to be one fucking mess. Bring the priest down. If he doesn't need medical attention, bring him to the station, arrest him, and book him."

A fireman called out, "Her head is in the backseat."

"Jesus Christ!" Detective John said. "We've got to get these bodies to the hospital even though they're dead."

"Sure," the sergeant said. "As long as we can reach 'em and get 'em out before the truck comes to lift the car off."

Someone cut the wire to silence the Cadillac's horn, ending the blaring noise as abruptly and violently as their lives had ended.

CHAPTER 148

YONKERS GENERAL HOSPITAL was clamoring with police, firemen, doctors, and emergency personnel as the lobby started to fill with reporters hearing the news on their police scanners. This was going to make headlines.

Within an hour, Charlie and Elaine arrived with a police escort from Manhattan.

Flashbulbs lit the lobby, making the sky appear as if it were on fire.

Charlie's face was pale and his countenance frightened. Elaine held Charlie's arm as they both rushed past the crowd that was shouting questions. They ignored the crowd and headed toward an open door, seeing Detective John in the doorway waiting for them. Izzy, Vince, and Bill Sullivan were not far behind, arriving within minutes. The only news that was given to them all when they were called and notified was that Michael and Regina had been in an automobile accident and were in Yonkers General Hospital.

The hospital's medical examiner was there to explain the details that no one was prepared to hear. When Elaine heard that both Michael and Regina were dead and that Regina's head had been cut off, she had to run to the sink to throw up. Charlie just sat there in silence. Vince stood next to Charlie, his hand on Charlie's shoulder, showing care in comforting him. In an instant, the king and queen were dead, and a new king was enthroned. Charlie stood and thanked the doctor, asking him for some privacy with his family as Maria, Frank, and Theresa arrived. Detective John gave Charlie the details.

Charlie turned to Izzy, Vince, and Bill.

"Priest or no priest, he will pay for his ungodly deed. Understand?" Charlie said.

CHAPTER 149

THEIR DEATHS MADE national news headlines: "INDUSTRIALIST MILLIONAIRE MICHAEL PELL AND WIFE KILLED IN TRAGIC AUTOMOBILE ACCIDENT BY DRUNK-DRIVING PRIEST!"

The obituary was concise, per the Pell Global Group's instructions.

Mr. and Mrs. Pell were friends of the US government and the many people who loved them, donating money and resources to those in need. Mr. Pell arrived in this country from Italy at the age of twelve, becoming one of the nation's most revered people, never passing a fifth grade level of schooling. Mrs. Pell was a devoted daughter, sister, wife, and mother, volunteering for many charities and helping to raise money, always giving of herself.

Over the years, the Pell Group supplied the US Army with fruit at little to no cost, helping the cause during World War II. Their holdings include wine and whiskey distributing and supplying produce nationally, in addition to mega real estate holdings throughout the country, including a hotel in Miami, Florida. Their businesses employ thousands of individuals.

Michael Pell and wife, Regina, are survived by their only son, Charles Nicholas Pell. Regina Pell is survived by her two sisters, Theresa Cappelli and Maria Abruzzi, and Maria's husband, Frank.

The funeral service is being held at Costa's Funeral Home on Henry Street, Lower Manhattan, with a Catholic Solemn Pontifical Mass[3] to follow at Our Lady of Fatima Church, Bronx, New York.

.

---

3   The Catholic Mass is the complex order of prayers and ceremonies celebrated by a bishop that make up the service of the sacrament in the Latin rites.

CHAPTER 150

THE STREETS SURROUNDING Our Lady of Fatima church were closed with police barricades so the funeral cortege would have some semblance of order. The church was packed, every seat filled with family, friends, and political and business associates who had to be accompanied by state troopers, police, and private bodyguards. No room was available for any one else to sit or stand. The crowd flowed to the outside steps and sidewalk, so the huge oak church doors were left open to let anyone standing outside hear some of what was going on inside. The press was not allowed inside, however. They waited outside wherever they could find a spot. Some even climbed telephone poles to snap their pictures.

One reporter was overheard saying, "I've covered a lot of stories but nothing like this. There has to be at least a thousand people here."

Bishop Joseph Zimarino, who had officiated the wedding ceremony for Regina and Michael, conducted the Solemn Pontifical Mass for their death in the same church with all its pomp and regalia. He wore his high gold hat and purple-and-gold gloves, along with green-and-gold vestige to cover a white robe. He carried his scepter as the smoke of burning incense gave the odor of sanctity.[1]

It was becoming a long, drawn-out day, with everyone trying to hear Bishop Zimarino over the humming of the large floor fans placed strategically against the perimeter of the walls. The bishop read from the holy book in front of him, partially reading and at some intervals singing in Latin. Getting the two

---

1 Odor of sanctity refers to the state of an individual's soul at the time of death. Some canonized saints are said to have died in an odor of sanctity.

handmade, engraved, mahogany caskets back out to the front of the church for the ride to Woodlawn Cemetery after the ceremony promised to be an arduous undertaking. So the police guard decided to take the caskets and family through a side door, where the funeral coach and limousines were already lined up and waiting.

CHAPTER 151

CHARLIE ARRANGED THE purchase of a huge mausoleum that would eventually hold fourteen caskets. In addition to his parents being buried there, he was going to move his four grandparents' bodies. When the time came, he and Elaine would be placed in the mausoleum, with room for additional family. The procession was so long, there had to be police escorts both in cars and on motorcycles.

The lead car carried the bishop with the funeral director, followed by four separate flower cars, two funeral coach cars carrying the caskets, the limousines carrying the immediate family, and an additional forty-eight limousines carrying friends and dignitaries.

The ceremonial graveside service ended with the church choir singing a hymn and the bishop closing with a prayer, immediately followed by a last private word to the family. Bishop Zimarino approached Charlie, embracing him with a traditional kiss to each cheek. The bishop knew he had an obligation to fulfill for all the help Michael's parents had given him and the church. And of course, he didn't want to lose Charlie as a contact.

Leaning into Charlie's right cheek with a kiss, he whispered, "Father LaRousse, originally from Monaco." Switching sides, the bishop leaned into Charlie's left cheek with a kiss, whispering, "Niya, Italy." Pulling away, he held Charlie with both hands, looking him in the eye.

"Bless you and may God be on your side," the bishop said, turning to walk back to the waiting car.

It only took a moment for Charlie to realize that Bishop Zimarino had just given up the drunken priest that had caused his parents' horrific deaths and where he could be found. The archdiocese had transferred him to Italy within days, thinking it would take years for the Pell family to find him.

CHAPTER 152

IT TOOK WEEKS for the dust to settle and get everyone back on track, but eventually it was business as usual, or as close as it could be under the circumstances.

Charlie's cousin Benevento with his parents, Adonis and Mechelina, left the Riverdale mansion and returned to Italy, but not before Charlie spoke to Benevento about his upcoming trip to Italy and how Benevento could repay the favor owed to Charlie for helping him many years ago. Without hesitation, Benny agreed and said he would have everything in place by the time Charlie arrived.

CHAPTER 153

Izzy, Vince, and Bill Sullivan were having breakfast at Empire Deli when Izzy brought up his concern about the future of their organization.

"I'm concerned about Charlie being able to handle having the keys to the kingdom," he said.

Bill lowered the morning paper, looking at Izzy with an expression that said, *What the fuck are you talking about?*

"No one has to worry about anything," Vince said. "He can handle it for sure."

"Why do you say that, Vince?" Izzy asked. "We have a right to know. I know that all things are now legit business and all, but it's a lot to handle. Look where he comes from and how he was raised."

Vince said, "He's a bright kid—"

Izzy interrupted him. "Yeah, I know he's smart, and he's not a kid. But what happens when it comes to the campaign and other shit he'll have to deal with?"

"Do you know why he and Elaine are going to Italy?" Vince asked. "He's going to find the priest."

"And when he finds him?"

"You're not fucking stupid, Izzy."

Vince leaned in, and both Izzy and Bill did the same.

"He's going to kill him," Vince said quietly. "What the fuck do you think he's going to do when he finds him? The bishop gave the priest up."

"Why didn't he get someone in Italy or even me?" Izzy asked.

"Well," Vince said, "let's think this through. It needs to be someone who will blend in, speak the language, and besides, Charlie wants to have a hands-on

— 273 —

hit. I know it sounds crazy, being in his position and all, and it looks like he is just so pissed that he wants to show his manhood and all that bullshit. But let me tell you this. He is willing to sacrifice whatever it will take to do what has to be done. You know as well as I do, Izzy, you would do the same. I know facts about Charlie and Elaine."

"What, what facts?" Bill asked.

"The fact that Charlie and Elaine rubbed out a few," Vince said.

Total silence fell over the table as the waiter attempted to take their order. Once that was done, Izzy said to the waiter, "And do not fucking sing."

Once the waiter scurried far enough away from the table to sing the order, Vince leaned in again to whisper.

"Charlie with his cousin Benevento in Italy and another he helped Elaine with. This will be his third and her second."

CHAPTER 154

WHEN CHARLIE AND Elaine arrived in Italy, they were met by Benny and a car and driver, who took them to the luxurious main house that was part of the winery where they would be staying. Adonis and Mechelina greeted them with open arms, welcoming Charlie back to Italy and embracing Elaine, even though it took much convincing by Benevento to have both Charlie and Elaine staying in the same bedroom when they were not married. One advantage both Charlie and Elaine had, was their knowledge of the Italian language, which certainly helped ease any tension between Adonis, Mechelina, and Elaine.

The first day was getting settled in and showing Elaine the winery. Elaine, being aware of their reason for traveling to Italy, was anxious to get the business at hand done as quickly as possible. Benny had to explain to her that although they had the needed information; things were done a little differently there.

"It can't be a slam, bam, thank you ma'am type of fucking," he said. "There are certain steps that have to be taken."

When Sophia walked into the batching area of the winery and saw Charlie and Elaine, she began talking in both Italian and English.

"Charlie, *i miei occhimi decieve me, e` davvero?*[1] All the way from America! *Permettetemi di salutarvi correttamente.*"[2] She gave Charlie a hug and a short kiss on the lips, then one on each cheek. "Ah! *Questa deve essere la ragazza Americana.*"[3]

---

1 Charlie do my eyes deceive me. Is it really you?

2 Let me greet you properly.

3 Ah! This must be the American girlfriend.

Charlie started to stammer as he attempted to introduce Sophia and Elaine. Just then, Elaine spoke up.

"*Io sono l'americano che è stato Charlies donne per anni. Sono contento che abbiamo finalmente incontriamo.*"[4]

Sophia, who was thrown by Elaine speaking in her native tongue, continued in English.

"Me too, Elaine. You a lucky people to have Charlie. Maybe we later all *mangiare insieme un pasto.*"[5]

---

4 I am the American who has been Charlie's woman for years. I'm glad we finally meet.
5 Eat a meal together.

CHAPTER 155

THE SMALL TOWN of Niya (pronounced Nee-a), Italy, sat right on the border between Switzerland and France, making it almost a full day's drive from Avellino.

Benny had arranged to use one of the small, unlettered winery trucks for them to travel in, so they wouldn't draw any attention to themselves, in addition to getting clothes for Charlie and Elaine that helped remain inconspicuous. Their distant cousin, Father Fredrico Paglia, arranged to have Father LaRousse at the church parish where he was now serving on a certain day and time, so he would not be visiting the townsfolk or the fields. He would often go to offer a blessing in return for wine.

Father LaRousse was known to say things like, "I can't wait for the day I get out of hell!" Of course, he meant the small town and the inconveniences he had to endure. Because of Father Paglia's communications with him and Father Paglia's connections with the archdiocese in Rome, LaRousse was under the impression that he was being visited to talk about a transfer to a larger city. He was looking forward to the "*legame comune di sacerdozio*"[1] and the chance to vent his disappointments.

Father Paglia traveled alone so he wouldn't have any connection with the threesome who were on a mission with only one goal...kill LaRousse

The town of Niya was well entrenched in tradition, family, and God. Its population was quite hardy. However, compared to New York, the town was quite sparse. Father LaRousse was not content with it all, particularly not being able to go to the local bars, since they were nonexistent. It was becoming a chore to find extra wine and whiskey to feed his demons.

---

1   Common bond of priesthood.

The table in the church basement was well arranged by LaRousse in anticipation his meeting that had one objective—get out of this hellhole of a town.

The conversation between Fathers LaRousse and Paglia was quite congenial, particularly since LaRousse was being plied with the whiskey Father Paglia had given him.

Father Paglia insisted LaRousse write a short note as a recompense for his carelessness that would help toward getting him perhaps to Rome. Father LaRousse found paper and pen and eagerly wrote a note.

"Mi dispiace per cio' che ho fatto, ho ucciso anime innocenti di mia mano. Non posso sopportare la vergogna. Perdonami."[2]
Padre LaRousse

Father Paglia assured LaRousse that this was the correct thing to do, and he promised to deliver this letter of sorrow and guilt to the correct person.

Hearing the faint sound of a vehicle coming to a stop, Father Paglia got up, excusing himself, LaRousse slurring incoherently. The three hurried down the basement stairs, passing Father Paglia as he was about to exit. He handed Benny the note LaRousse had just composed and signed.

"May God be with you all," he said. Not turning back to look, he left the church.

"Quick, the rope!" Benny said in English.

Elaine handed him the rope needed to complete the deed. "He's all yours, Charlie."

Father LaRousse tried to look up at his guests. "Ah, that was fast. You taking me to Roma?"

Charlie, without hesitation, went behind LaRousse with a piece of leather strap. He wrapped it around his neck, pulling as tight as he could.

"Stai andando a Roma bene," Charlie whispered. *"Morire per i tuoi peccati. Nel nome di mia madre e mio padre.* You're going to Rome all right. Die for your sins, in the name of my mother and father." At that moment, LaRousse brayed a

---

2 I am sorry for my deed killing innocent souls by my hand. I cannot stand the shame. Forgive me.

short, harsh noise until no more sound emerged. It took all three of them to lift LaRousse from the chair, hoisting him by his neck with the rope Elaine had given to Benny, to make it look as if he committed suicide by hanging himself.

Benny left the handwritten note by stabbing it to the table with LaRousse's knife. Elaine took the other plate, cup, and utensils that had been set for Father Paglia and put them back into a cabinet. At the last moment, Benny kicked the chair from under LaRousse's feet to set the scene.

Elaine grabbed Charlie to kiss him, rubbing her hand up and down his thigh. She felt him get hard.

"I wish we had time to stay and...Oh!" she said. "There's the smell!"

"Stop, now! We must go," Benny sternly interrupted. "They always shit their pants!"

CHAPTER 156

THE THREE DROVE through the night, only stopping along the way to bury the strap used to strangle LaRousse and to urinate. They were able to make it back to Avellino by sunrise to join in as the day began.

Charlie and Elaine promised each other they would make time to visit Mama's sister, Luisa, who was suffering from diabetes mellitus and had to have her leg amputated. Regina had been sending funds to her aunt to pay for all her medical necessities and the full-time home care. Pell Global Group continued to cover the costs.

The visit was not easy. Luisa would drift from clarity to being incoherent from the morphine she had to take for pain.

Charlie knew it was probably the last time he would see his great-aunt and tried to find some family history in her house, but to no avail. They stayed the night to see how the medical help handled Luisa before they said their last good-byes.

Elaine encouraged Charlie to take his aunt's advice, when she was lucid, and go to the town hall and seek whatever family records he could. All records were kept by the town's *ufficiale dello stato civile*,[1] along with church records. Early morning came and they said their farewells and headed to the town hall.

As they were searching, Elaine started to use her law school skills. She knew how to scan pages, quickly moving her finger left to right, scribbling notes as fast as her fingers allowed her. Her mind became bleary from hours

---

1 Journal of civil status.

of searching, reading, and writing extensive notes. She rubbed her eyes from exhaustion and shook Charlie to wake him up.

"Help me put these notes together," she said.

"Take them. We'll put them together tomorrow. We've been awake for hours. Let's go to the farmhouse and get some sleep," he pleaded. "We'll look at them tomorrow."

Grabbing the papers, which had notes and lines going in every direction, Elaine folded them, making a crumpling sound. She stuffed them into her blouse and agreed to leave.

CHAPTER 157

AFTER THEY TOOK a bath located in the main part of the house, one at a time so they wouldn't upset Adonis and Mechelina, Charlie fell asleep. Elaine kept the light low in their room so she could work on her notes. She was eager to surprise Charlie when he awoke.

By moving each name from one page to the master chart, she planned out a family tree. She crossed out a mistake she found in her scribbled notes, placing a date here and a date there and adding a comment to this name and a note to another person or date.

Finally she had the family chart ready for Charlie. As she read it from person to person, noting their names and how each was related, she stopped and stared with disbelief.

"No! No fucking way! Did I make a mistake?" She read the chart up and down, down and up, checking and rechecking her notes, before letting out a guttural sigh with barely enough energy to mutter, "Shit!"

Staring at the finished writing, she saw:

"We're cousins. Oh my God! Me, Charlie, and somewhere in there has got to be Benny. We're all fucking cousins."

Excited, she turned to Charlie, her chatter almost incoherent. "Charlie, we're cousins…We're related…does that make us have bad blood together? We can never have children!"

Elaine quietly removed her robe, looking at her soft, Mediterranean, olive skin and admiring what she saw in the mirror. She manipulated her breasts to watch her nipples rise, pushing her tits up to kiss them. Slowly moving to the bed, she gently pulled down the sheet to kneel so she could remove Charlie's

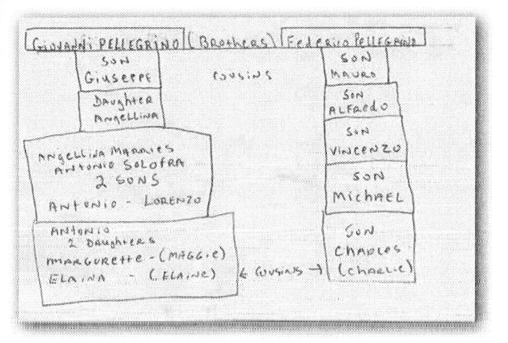

cock from his underwear. She put as much into her mouth as she could fit until it filled her. Charlie woke from his slumber.

"I've missed you," Elaine said. "I have a surprise for you." She took his underpants off and climbed on top, swinging her leg over with her back toward him. She gently inserted him into her welcoming, wet muff. Charlie got harder with each thrust, going deeper into Elaine. He called to mind how he'd taught her this position, which he'd picked up from the Grace Bar and Grill. Their movement took on its own tempo. Coming together, they had to be very quiet, holding in any sounds. The restraint made them both peak with even more excitement as Charlie's cock exploded with a pulsating flow of ejaculate.

"I love your surprises," Charlie said. Elaine turned to hold him, giving him quick kisses.

"I have more surprises. Did you ever notice how much we think alike—you, me, and Benevento?" Closing her eyes, sleepy now, she whispered, "Charlie, let's get married. Here in Italy. The priest, Paglia, can perform the ceremony. Isn't he a cousin too?" And then she dozed off.

CHAPTER 158

MONTHS PASSED. BOTH Charlie and Elaine had a newfound respect within the Pell Group, and for each other, since their marriage in Italy.

January 20 was an extremely cold day in Washington, DC, with a light snowfall.

Charlie and Elaine, with their Pell Global Group inner circle and their guests, were sitting among members of Congress, Supreme Court justices, high-ranking military officers, and former presidents, along with other dignitaries in the seating area in front of the nation's Capitol building.

The chief justice stood in front of a tall, handsome man, his wife next to him. The man placed his left hand on a Bible, held his right hand up to take his oath of office, and repeated the words as directed.

"I do solemnly swear that I will faithfully execute the office of President of the United States, and will to the best of my ability, to preserve, protect, and defend the Constitution of the United States."

The chief justice shook the hand of the newly inaugurated president and turned to the vast crowd, who was applauding and cheering.

"Ladies and gentleman of America, I introduce to you the president of theUnited States, Samuel Roberts, and first lady, Priscilla Roberts."

REFERENCES

Map of Italy; Google images; Freeworldmaps.net/Europe/Italy/Campania.htnl
Two prize fighters; Google Images

Song: "As Time Goes By"
Written by Herman Hupfeld in 1931

Song." Solo Per Te" (For You Alone)
Lyrics by P.J. O'Reilly
Music by Henry Egeehl 1909
Recorded by Enrico Caruso 1911

Song of praise sang while stomping grapes; Psalmist, fred berri

Italian translation: Austin Sanniota Edwards

ABOUT THE AUTHOR
fred berri

Thank you for reading my novel.

I hope you enjoyed it, and I look forward to seeing you in my next adventure.

fred berri

fred berri was born in the Bronx, New York, and moved to Yonkers. After graduating high school, he returned back into a section of the Bronx known as Little Italy.

Early in his career, he worked a wide variety of jobs, from grocery stock clerk, to retail manager of a large national variety store, each one teaching him something new. Eventually he started and sold his own business, which grew to employ more than a hundred people.

Over the years, berri has written a number of articles for trade publications and websites, and he has given several newspaper interviews about his business.

A seasoned public speaker, he has done television voiceover work and held live seminars to help others achieve their biggest goals. He is also the website creator and founder of http://www.RetirementUSA.com.

Currently retired, ending a long career as a financial specialist with one of the largest banking institutions in the United States, berri lives in South Florida, which he has called home for more than a quarter of a century.

COUSINS' BAD BLOOD